AN
ANTHOLOGY
EDITED BY
ANDREW WINCH

WARRIORS AGAINST THE STORM

DEDICATED TO **MARY WEBER**
AUTHOR AND TEACHER EXTRAORDINAIRE

Mt Zion Ridge Press LLC
295 Gum Springs Rd, NW
Georgetown, TN 37366

https://www.mtzionridgepress.com

ISBN 13: 978-1-949564-87-7

Published in the United States of America
Publication Date: October 15, 2020

Editor-In-Chief: Andrew Winch

Cover Art Copyright by Kirk DouPounce © 2020

All rights reserved. No portion of this book may be reproduced or transmitted in any form or by any electronic or mechanical means, including photocopying, recording or by any information retrieval and storage system without permission of the publisher.

Ebooks, audiobooks, and print books are *not* transferrable, either in whole or in part. As the purchaser or otherwise *lawful* recipient of this book, you have the right to enjoy the novel on your own computer or other device. Further distribution, copying, sharing, gifting or uploading is illegal and violates United States Copyright laws. Pirating of books is illegal. Criminal Copyright Infringement, *including* infringement without monetary gain, may be investigated by the Federal Bureau of Investigation and is punishable by up to five years in federal prison and a fine of up to $250,000.

Names, characters and incidents depicted in this book are products of the author's imagination, or are used in a fictitious situation. Any resemblances to actual events, locations, organizations, incidents or persons – living or dead – are coincidental and beyond the intent of the author.

DEDICATION

Warriors Against the Storm is a group project sponsored by Havok Publishing and Mt. Zion Ridge Press in tribute to author **Mary Weber**, who has made us—her army of fans and friends in the writing community—stronger and wiser in ways that even we can't fully describe.

Along with being the award-winning, multi-published young adult author of *The Storm Siren Trilogy, The Evaporation of Sofi Snow* series, and *To Best the Boys*, Mary has spent years pouring selflessly into others as a youth pastor, speaker, advocate, and writing mentor. And now it's our turn to pour into *her*. With this project, we will support Mary and her family as she weathers the storm that has taken her home and health through mold poisoning. All profits of the Anthology will bless Mary and her family directly.

How the Anthology Came to Life
A note from Elizabeth Van Tassel and Lauren Brandenburg

It's not often you meet someone who's a powerful force for good. Every time you read her stories or connect at a conference, Mary leaves others inspired with a fresh perspective. When I heard about their loss of home and wellbeing, I (Elizabeth) was devastated. As a wildfire survivor who lost everything in one night, I also have had to close the door on a home and never return to it—and start over again, with no clothes or belongings. I know what it's like having mounting bills and no place of our own, yet the unexpected kindness of so many touched us deeply. In gratitude to the many who once helped us, I reached out and offered to help Mary's family. Others came together and we formed Weber's Warriors, a public group on Facebook of fans and friends in the writing community who wanted to make a difference.

The group started small, with boosts on social media and giveaways organized by her writing community, and then…a special offer arrived out of the blue. Not one, but two publishers would band together to each offer their expertise to compile an anthology dedicated to Mary as a fundraiser. First, Lauren Brandenburg—who had her own story of rebuilding after devastating financial loss—came on board to help with Weber's Warriors and the Anthology efforts.

Since then, we've had a team of amazing volunteers who were willing to jump right in and keep the momentum going despite the COVID-19 pandemic and other challenges. The team at Havok, including editor Andrew Winch, Teddi Deppner, and Lisa Gefrides all have been a wonder to watch as they bring out their magic and dedication to building beautiful, composite stories and hosting the *Warriors* contest on their website. Michelle Levigne had the idea to begin with and has brought the vision to life with Tamera Lynn Kraft and Mt. Zion Ridge Press is helping to bring it to print. Kirk DouPonce captured the spirit of the work and designed an amazing cover. Finally, Jeane Wynn offered her expertise with publicity needs as the project grew into a world-changing movement far beyond any of our individual efforts.

I've loved watching this creation of faith and hope develop and continue during a time when we all need it the most. Thank you for being part of something special to help this wonderful family with amazing stories of renewed hope.

TABLE OF CONTENTS

DUST DANCER
Jason C. Joyner   1

LIGHTNING IN A BOTTLE
Lani Forbes   9

ONE MORE DAY
Clint Hall   17

SPIRIT OF THE JAGUAR
Cassandra Hamm   25

THE STORMS OF POSEIDON
Patrick M. Fitzgerald   33

THE REVEALING
E.S. Marsh   41

THE GUARDIAN'S MELODY
Zachary Holbrook   49

THE HEART OF A SHADOW
Tracey Dyck   57

DRIFT
Roystonn Pruitt   65

THE UGLY CRONE
Karen Avizur   73

THE PLAGUE DRAGON
J.L. Ender   81

DREAMS AND NIGHTMARES
Luna R. Fuhrman   89

HOLD
Emily Hayse   97

THE NIGHT BEASTS
Savannah Grace   105

ONE FOOT IN THE GRAVE
SCE Swayne   113

AFTER THE WAR
Emily Grant   121

STORMS OF THE HEART
Laura L. Zimmerman   129

THE SWITCH
Rebecca Waddell   137

THE DOLL GIRL
Sarah Stasik   145

A PLACE AMONG THE STARS
Cassia Schaar   153

About the Editor   160

DUST DANCER
Jason C. Joyner

"When the dust settles, my sweet Gabri, that's when you see the truth."

I remind myself of one of the few things I remember my mum saying before I settled into the service of my mistress. Now I scrub the tiles of her portico while an ocean breeze makes my hair dance around my face. The cooling wind eases the ache of my muscles and the burn of my most recent marks

Alina enters with drinks for our masters, her tiny shoulders slumped. I try to take the hard tasks to save the younger girl such trouble. She hands a delicate container to Lady Vara, who loves nothing more than to make people squirm by controlling them.

"Did you forget the appetizer for your lord?" My mistress scowls. "Goodness, girl, get on with it."

Quickly, Alina sets a larger mug on the porcelain table for Lord Marcillieus. He growls and swats at her, causing her to stumble. My anger flares; the girl's only nine seasons, and slight for her age. My fist tightens, but Alina scampers off before I seal my own fate.

"We're due for a visit to the capital for more shopping, darling." Lady Vara coos in a sing-song tone to soothe her husband. A long finger with a decorated nail skims the rim of her glass.

My lord empties his cup in one swallow and slams it down. In the lowering sun, I see the dust motes dancing in the air, thrust from their slumber to ride the yellow rays back down to their resting place.

The dust never lies.

"We have all we require right now. Why, if we attained more goods, we'd have to build a new wing to the villa," Lord Marcillieus states as if it's the end of the subject.

I spare a glance at my mistress to see her eyes narrow

slightly, a hardening of the jaw line. This isn't what she wanted to hear. How will she react?

Alina enters with a tray containing the appetizer for the next hour. Her thin linen dress clings to her small frame while she tries to balance the serving dishes on her tray. As she sets it on the table, Lady Vara moves her foot just enough to make Alina stumble.

A serving dish of chilled shrimp and lemon wedges tips towards Lord Marcillieus. His muscular arm moves to steady it, but the drink has dulled his reflexes. Fingers catch the edge of the circular table and flip it over. Its top splinters into several pieces while the food and drink splatter all over the portico.

My heart drops, not for the labor I'll have to repeat, but for poor Alina's fate. A snarl crosses Lord Marcillieus's face, and a rough hand locks onto her tiny arm. I sit up, intent on standing up for her this time, but a fierce glare from my mistress silences me. Again.

"Fool girl," he spits. "Look what you've done. Now I'll have to travel to the capital for a new table. Your hide will be part of the payment. I weary of your clumsy ways."

Alina whimpers as he drags her out of the gateway, but she doesn't cry out, to deprive him of some satisfaction. I'm proud of her for that. My mind races to the rocky coastline that this villa is nestled next to and the spindly trees that fight for purchase between the crevices. Trees with lower branches that die with each passing spring, making them perfect switches to add marks to wayward servants.

My own scars sting with every cry from Alina as I clean up the mess under the smirking gaze of Lady Vara.

❧❧❧

With the evening dishes finally put away, I hope to escape and slip to my bedroll unnoticed, but not tonight. Lady Vara beckons for me from the veranda outside.

I stop next to a small patch of sand under a flowering bush. The scent from the blossoms would be pleasing to most people, but I only associate it with sadness and anger.

"Gabri, we need some entertainment to put us in the proper mood. I want Marcillieus well rested for the travel ahead tomorrow."

Lady Vara dances her fingertips over her husband's neck, softening his sullen mood. He is not interested in what I have to offer, but it may put Lady Vara in the proper mindset to satisfy his desires this evening.

My bare feet sense the rough grains scattered over the cooling tiles. The setting sun creates the light that best illuminates my gift. The golden hour, as my mistress calls it.

I reach out with my hands, fingers splayed to feel the connection to the bits of dust, visible not by eye but by gift. The larger grains in my vicinity tremble as I reach out and meld with every piece.

A twirl of my hand sends a stream of sand leaping up onto a pedestal. The different threads of dust swirl together until I form them into two people dancing together. I even make the man act dashing by holding out a tiny flower to the woman. Sweat beads on my forehead as I make the figures as full and lifelike as I can. Does my mistress approve? I dare not glance her way and risk losing my concentration.

The grainy dancers spin. I make the woman fall down into a pile, only to spring up above the male figure. Knowing that Lord Marcillieus is cross tonight, and Lady Vara is intent on playing him out, I push all I can into the performance.

It isn't until I hear their steps fade in the distance and my mistress's giggles echo through the night that I dare let the dust fall.

Will I see her footprints in the morning, signs that she left their chambers to find another's comfort? Or will it be *his* turn to sneak out?

The dust never lies.

༄༄༄

Before I slip to my thin bedding, I climb a wall to look over the rocky outcropping that juts into the sea. Their villa, nestled into the peninsula, provides a spectacular view of the waters. A frail moon reflects a silvery thread across the gentle waves.

Alina grunts as she climbs up next to me. My instinct is to put my arm around her, but I cannot see where her new marks are, so I do not risk it. Still, her silent presence comforts me. She is like the sister I never had.

"Why do they have to be so cruel?" Alina breathes out the

words. When we meet at night, we must avoid being caught, or we may find ourselves tossed into the breakers.

Once again I swear to protect her instead of sitting by in silent cowardice. "Who knows what torment goes on in their heads to treat others so poorly? I hope we can learn to be brave and kind instead of going through life releasing such poison."

My adopted sister leans her head on my shoulder. I reach back with my other arm and call up some dust to give her a simple gift of joy. Two little girls of sand join hands and stroll into the night, into freedom.

༄༄༄

The morning chores call with the sunrise. I stretch my body out and mouth a silent prayer that today will be different. My ritual since I was five seasons old. I have not skipped a day in nine seasons now.

After eating a small orange and a piece of flatbread, I begin the laundry. I'm surprised when Lady Vara snaps at me to join her and the master immediately.

I scamper to the barn to find Alina in a tunic and trousers, with a strip of cloth wrapped around her mouth. Only her eyes are able to speak, a torrent of fear and confusion spilling out from her verdant irises.

"You two, get in the back of the wagon. It is a lengthy trip to where we're going," Lord Marcillieus says wearily.

We have never gone with them on a journey before. Alina and I share a confused glance while taking our place on the rear bench, hanging over the passing ground as the horses lead us out to the fine gravel road.

Unrelenting sunshine beats down against my skin, turning my shoulders red. Sweat dampens the wrap across Alina's face. Or is it her tears? My hand finds hers, and I give it a squeeze.

As we continue on, the villa's dried grasses and low scrub bushes give way to dunes decorated with wind-swept curls at the top. An ocean of sand surrounds us as the horses pull the wagon through the desolate panorama.

I've never seen anything so beautiful.

I'd always struggled to comprehend the idea of a desert. All that sand in one place. Dust twirling on its own in the wind, shaping the land for leagues. The villa is surrounded by unforgiving rocks, not unending sand. It was beyond a dream to see it, and now it calls to me.

I can feel every speck, each grain begging for me to send it dancing. My fingers tingle with anticipation, and my breath catches as I imagine the show I could display.

My thoughts stutter to a stop as the wagon brakes. I realize we've come across an incredible sight. In the midst of the ripples and dunes, a grouping of trees surrounds a blue splash of water. Other wagons, draped with brightly colored curtains, stand at one side of the pool. A small bazaar shelters under the trees. Lord Marcillieus steps down and offers a hand to Lady Vara.

A moment later, a group of men approaches, their smeared faces and ragged beards making my heart race. The dirt they track with each heavy step reveals their thirst for destruction. Decay litters each footstep. The dust never lies.

The fine granules that coat my clothing vibrate and rise ever so slightly. As my breath catches, my hand rolls the grime into a spinning ball in my palm, growing slowly with each passing moment.

Hushed whispers flow between my masters and these men. I can't make out the words, but when they gesture to the wagons already gathered at the water's edge, I see a shaking of the dust on the curtains covering the wagons. Yet there's no wind to stir the air.

The motes rippling in the air match a group of people breathing in and out. Then I notice a small head peering out from the rear, eyes wide as the girl spies on the men. Her gaunt features and wide eyes confirm what I'd feared. These men are here to hurt people.

Their words grow animated as Lord Marcillieus gestures toward Alina and me. I catch Lady Vara's gaze before she turns and puts a hand on the lord's arm. She leans to his ear, whispering to him.

After a few more exchanges, Lord Marcillieus grasps hands with the lead man, and they all retreat to their wagons. Circling around, my lord faces the two of us on our perch.

"Looks like I get to shorten my trip with these traders," he says with a grin. Pointing to me, he says, "Milady values you too much. But we bartered well enough to convince them *she's* worth the trade."

My mouth gapes as he takes Alina over his shoulder in one fell swoop.

"You stay put," he says, "or I'll take Vara's wrath and rid myself of you, too."

Alina's eyes go wide, but the rag keeps her voice silenced. She squirms in his grip, which only earns her a slap. I jump down from the bench, ready to cry out.

Lady Vara stalks over to me, her face tight. "She is not worth the trouble. Be thankful I felt your worth high enough to continue enduring your failings. Get back on the wagon."

My little sister. They *can't* take her away from me. I must not hide again from doing what is right.

Before I realize it, my hand opens to reveal the ball I've formed. My mistress sneers at my feeble offering, until a twitch of my fingers gives it a pointed edge. With a flick, it strikes her throat.

Lady Vara grasps at the wound, but I make the sand dissolve and drop into her lungs. I run past her as she stumbles to her knees. The innumerable grains listen to my plea, and a dust storm whips up in front of me. With a shout, I skid between Lord Marcillieus and the foul traders.

Instead of mustering dainty, dancing figures, I command entire waves of earth, from fine powder to coarse grit. My weapon wraps around Marcillieus's legs and yanks him down. He lets Alina go while scrambling to pull himself free from the consuming dune.

"Run to our wagon, Alina!" My voice stirs her to action.

The traders holler in shock. They pull weapons from their belts and try to move around me. My arms circle in the air, directing streams of granules to flood their faces. Each of them chokes while the air swirls with silt, filling their lungs and silencing their voices.

I let the dust dance around me until nothing else moves, and finally it, too, settles to the ground. Scattered limbs stick out from the sandy graveyard. I glance to the dune where my lord disappeared. Lady Vara stares at me with unseeing eyes, her body lying motionless.

My breath is ragged. What have I done? Thoughts race as I

consider what was necessary to save Alina. She pulls off the cloth and runs to me, sobbing. I catch her in my arms and try to wipe the dirt streaks from her cheeks, but her tears make new trails down her face. Tremors shake my body as I realize why I had to act. I fall to my knees, trying to keep my heart from shattering.

Movement catches my eye. A few other children slip out of the wagon, looking around with wonder in their eyes. The oldest one, a boy near my age, steps forward and scans the remains of the traders. "What happened to them?"

My throat catches. "Did they hurt you?"

He nods.

My eyes cloud with tears. Despite the cost to my soul, all of us face a new day. "They won't hurt you anymore. Neither will my masters hurt us." I brush Alina's curly hair back from her forehead, offering her a gentle smile.

"How do you know?" she asks.

"The dust never lies."

LIGHTNING IN A BOTTLE
Lani Forbes

The first sign was always a shift in the wind. The towering palms that lined the cliffs would bend at the waist as though seasick. Then, the waves crashing below would grow, taking out their rage upon the rocks.

Cora watched the first flashes of lighting crackle against the dark clouds gathering on the horizon. The wind whipped her dark hair back from her face, and the tang of salt filled her nose. With each burst of distant light, hope burned hotter within her chest.

The first storm of the season.

In the township below, the ramshackle collection of wooden houses and shops already buzzed with activity. The energy guild ships bobbed alongside the rowboats of common fisherman—whales beside minnows both in size and sophistication. Metal collection nets already stretched out across the riggings, silver spiderwebs waiting for power instead of morning dew.

Cora jingled the watt coins in her coat pocket, their sparks snapping reassuringly at her fingers, storing the last bits of energy she and her mother had saved up before the dry season.

Just enough to buy Cora's passage on a real guild ship.

She sprinted back to the stone cottage, almost tripping over her leather boots with excitement. She threw open the wooden door with a bang that shook the dust from the rafters.

"First storm of the season!" She announced.

Her mother continued to poke at the pot suspended over the fireplace as if she had not heard. Finally, she stood and wiped her hands on the stained apron around her waist, the fabric as weather beaten and wrinkled as her face.

"Cor, I thought we talked about this. There's no way they're going to let you on one of the guild ships, even if you spend every watt we've saved since your father died."

But Cora was already digging through her father's old sea

chest, throwing aside maps and charts, looking for his old collection supplies. "I have to try. This storm is going to be a big one. I can feel it."

The single electric lamp that lit their one-room cottage flickered, its energy beginning to run low. They'd already resorted to cooking over the fireplace again.

"Why can't you just learn to sew like the other girls in town? Offer to mend the lightningers cloaks and earn some wattage that way."

Cora's fingers found the finely woven metal net. It unfurled in her hands, slightly tinged with rust but sturdy enough for her purposes. Next, she gathered two empty glass bottles with rubber stoppers, the kind her mother usually reserved for milk. "Because we both know my needlework is shoddy, at best."

Her mother eyed the empty milk bottles then the leather breeches Cora wore beneath her father's old, blue coat. She clucked her tongue. "Don't complain to me when they chuck you out of the guild's office. They'll reject you the same as they did your father."

Cora's stomach clenched. She knew she shouldn't expect approval. She had never been good at the things her mother deemed appropriate for a young woman. *You can't lose something you never had to begin with.*

Cora shoved the mesh net and bottles into a satchel bag and threw it over her shoulder. "Wish me luck." She tucked her long hair up into one of her father's caps.

Her mother continued to poke at the fire. "You're not going to catch anything, even if they let you on."

Cora straightened her spine and began her march down the hill. She couldn't let her mother's doubts drag her down. They would drown her if she let them.

The streets bustled with guild lightningers and fishermen alike, all hauling supplies to the ships setting sail before the storm made landfall. The red brick guild office stood out sore and imposing like a swollen thumb. The squat wooden buildings beside it, a brothel and lawyer's office, seemed to lean away as if afraid of guilt by association.

"I'd like to purchase passage on the *Tenebris*." Cora slapped her silver watt coins onto the polished, wooden, front desk.

The older man surveyed her over his spectacles, his powdered wig perfectly quaffed and absorbing the light of the many electric lamps shining overhead. "Name?"

"Cora." She chewed her tongue for the briefest of moments. "Cora Clarke."

"Clarke?" Amusement tugged at the corner of the man's thin lips. "Hmm."

His gloved fingers lifted one of the silver coins as if inspecting its authenticity. Her pulse thrashed inside her veins as she waited for his verdict.

"I'm afraid the price for passage has gone up for non-guild members. It will be twenty watts."

Cora clenched her teeth. "Twenty? You're making that up. You charged the man ahead of me twelve for passage on the same ship!"

"Yes." He withdrew a kerchief from his pocket and polished his spectacles. "And his last name was Rogers."

"And that matters because?" She nearly stomped her foot but resisted.

"Because." He looked up and smirked. "He is not a Clarke."

Cora wished she could bottle the lightning crackling in her gaze as she stomped from the office. Just because her father had spoken out against the guild's monopoly on the energy market, which was essentially speaking against the crown itself, they would never give her a real chance. Her father might pay for his crime for the rest of his life in one of the kingdom's dungeons, but she would be the one to forever bear his shame.

As she strode out onto the bustling docks, the wind picked up, pulling greedily at the king's flag atop the guild office. The sky continued to darken. She could keep fighting, keep trying to force her way into a world that didn't want her... or she could forge her own path entirely.

Just as her father had done.

It wasn't her preferred path, but it was now the only one she had left.

Beneath the fancy wooden docks, beneath the polished shoes and powdered wigs, the beach concealed a darker world — a world where a bribe or a threat would buy your way onto a boat without question. Granted, the common fishing vessels run by the black-market pirates were as likely to transport you to the bottom of the sea as to your desired shore.

Lucky for Cora, Benjamin owed her a favor.

Her boots sank into the cool, dark sand as the dock's shadow closed over her head. A line of about twenty boats of various sizes and states of shabbiness lined up along the water's edge like bloated, beached whales. Several of the rogue fishermen worked at rigging makeshift collection nets to their sails, though most little were more than stray wires twisted together. The guild might control the best ships, but they couldn't claim ownership over the sea itself, no matter how much they wanted to.

Cora found the faded, blue boat with a dolphin painted across its starboard side. She kicked it to get its owner's attention.

"Oy!" Benjamin turned around, his black coat flapping like the overgrown bat he resembled, his stormy eyes as gray as the sky above. "What in the name of the goddess' great, green—"

"Don't finish that sentence or she may strike you dead where you stand." Cora crossed her arms. The corner of her mouth quirked up in a teasing grin. Benjamin was only older than her by two years, but the weight he carried on his lonely shoulders sometimes made the gap feel much larger.

"No." He offered nothing further before turning back to untangle his fishing nets.

"You promised. I saved your skin with those guards, and you told me any time I needed a favor—"

Benjamin threw his nets down. "A favor like saving some extra fish for you out of my next catch! Not risking my life so you can pretend to be a lightninger."

"I'm not pretending. I'm going to catch some."

Benjamin rolled his eyes. "With what? You think you can attract the watts with your charming personality?"

Cora stuck out her tongue. "Fine, then I can always tell the guards *exactly* how you manage to get out of paying the docking tax."

His hand rubbed at his temple. "You don't even have—"

But Cora had already pulled out her father's old collection net and held it up.

Benjamin sighed.

"I have two bottles. If I catch some, I'll give you half."

A spark of interest ignited in his eyes. "Half? That's at least ten thousand-watt coins."

"A year's worth of wages, I'd reckon." She swung the net tauntingly in front of his face, a charmer before a snake.

Benjamin fingered the edge of his empty fishing net, which was a darker, wetter shade of brown than normal, meaning he'd already used it and come up empty-handed. Again.

"Fine," he said. "But we're coming back in the *minute* the waves get too rough. If I lose this boat, it'll be more than a year's wages."

Cora beamed. "Perfect."

"You're as stubborn as a starfish," Benjamin said, rubbing at his temple again.

Cora climbed into the boat and unfolded her father's old collection rod until it stood as tall as a mast, then began stringing up her metal net.

Benjamin heaved the boat into the choppy waters and took to the oars. His thin frame rowed them out into the harbor with surprising efficiency as Cora wobbled toward the front. She removed her cap, letting her hair and face soak in the cool spray that sprang up whenever the bow of the boat smacked against a whitecap.

With each swell's dip, she heard their criticisms, the doubts of her mother and everyone else. *You're not going to catch anything, even if they let you on.* An image swam behind her eyelids of the old man from the guild scrunching his nose at her. *Because he is not a Clarke.* Then, with each rise, she drowned out their voices with the only one that mattered — the voice that believed in her and told her she could do whatever she set her mind to.

The voice of her father.

"Why can't you just make money the same way the other girls in town do?" Benjamin huffed with heavy breaths between each stroke of the oars.

Cora glanced down at her breeches. "I'm not *like* the other girls in town." It was a fact everyone seemed determined to remind *her* of. Why was it so hard for *them* to understand?

"I just don't think this is only about the money for you."

Cora spun around and glared at him. "What is *that* supposed to mean?"

"I'm just saying, you could make plenty doing something else. Baking bread with Mrs. Porter, sewing and seamstressing like Ms. Kent. They do fine without blackmailing honest, hardworking fisherman to take them out in the middle of a storm."

She arched a brow at him. "Maybe it *isn't* just about the money."

Benjamin's lips curled into a knowing smile. "It never is."

The waves grew steeper, and with them the doubting voices in her head grew louder. With each dip down into the valley, it was getting hard and harder to pull herself back up. Benjamin gritted his teeth as he fought to keep the small boat steady. Thunder boomed across the waters as loud as cannon blasts.

"I'm not sure we can stay out here much longer," he called just as drops of heavy rain began to pelt their faces.

"Just a little farther!" Cora yelled back. "We don't need to get to the center, just close enough for lightning to strike."

"You're going to get us both killed, and then I am going to kill you." Benjamin's threat sounded too much like a promise, but miraculously, he kept rowing.

The clouds churned as thick as black oil above them. Ahead, stray lightning bolts struck the turbulent waves. A fish bobbed past them on the surface, its dead, bulging eyes warning Cora to turn back.

Instead, she inspected her equipment with trembling fingers as the cold rain crept through her gloves. The rod and net were set exactly as her father had always showed her, both of the net's collection lines running into one of the glass bottles.

Then it happened.

The bolt of lightning illuminated the sky in flaming pinks and violets. As blinding light connected with the rod, sparks danced out from the center and along the fibers of the collection net. The expanding air cracked so loud around Cora that she wondered if her ears might bleed. Benjamin held his arms over his head and shouted something, but she couldn't hear him over the ringing.

And then, it was over as quickly as it came, and Cora's gaze dropped to the bottles on the boat deck. She pulled the rubber stoppers out of her pocket and jammed them into their mouths, effectively containing thousands of watts of sparkling, violet-white energy

As the ringing faded from her ears, she choked out a sigh of relief. Benjamin finally lowered his arms and stared at her with a mixture of horror and wonder. He then carefully lifted one of the bottles, turning it this way and that, marveling as the natural beauty of the power contained within.

"You did it," he said softly. "No offense, but I didn't know…"

Cora swiped a tear from her cheek. "I did."

And she *had* known. Because she knew she was not destined to sew buttons or bake bread. That she was destined for something so much greater, so much more than anyone else left in her life could imagine. "Before he was taken, my dad taught me the greatest secret there is to catching lighting in a bottle."

"What's that?" Benjamin asked, taking up the oars again.

Cora smiled as she quoted from memory, imagining the wrinkles that had creased the corners of her father's eyes. "'They will laugh at you and tell you that you'll fail. They will question your judgment, even your sanity. You won't have the right training, the right friends, the right tools. But go anyway. Go because you have to. Go because you know you'll regret it every minute for the rest of your life if you don't. Go because the payoff might be worth the risk in the end. You see, my child, the hardest thing about catching lightning in a bottle isn't catching the lightning at all."

ONE MORE DAY
Clint Hall

The warrior rose up on his toes as he laid his golden-haired son into the crib, twisting his aching body so the handle of his sword wouldn't knock against the wooden rail. He never dared to remove the weapon from his hip, not after darkness fell. He couldn't risk it being out of reach when the attack came.

And it came every night.

On the nightstand, a machine shaped like an owl produced white noise under the sound of a heartbeat. A wet spot warmed the left side of the warrior's shirt where his son's mouth had lain against his chest. It had taken nearly two hours to soothe the child to sleep tonight.

Too long. The warrior blamed himself as he tiptoed between the chewed board books and mismatched toy cars scattered across the floor. Despite his attempts to calm his mind and focus his breathing while rocking his son, he suspected that the infant could sense his tormented thoughts. That was unacceptable, and as the warrior eased shut the door—covered with the same thick mattress foam that adorned the walls—he vowed to do better tomorrow night.

If he was still alive.

The warrior ascended the carpeted stairs, skipping the step that always creaked beneath his weight. A pain like searing hot needles jabbed at his mind. The sensation occurred whenever the creatures were close. He had to hurry.

Another door—padded and padlocked—waited at the top of the stairs. He paused to listen for his son, for a telltale whimper or possibly the same innocent gibberish that escaped the boy's mouth when he crawled across the floor, pushing his cars. The warrior heard nothing. *Good.*

A cold, dead air greeted him as he opened the door and moved into the main level of the farmhouse. Dusty floorboards groaned beneath his boots as he eased toward the front door.

Moonlight seeped in between the wood planks that covered the windows, but how, he didn't know. He had spent many daylight hours nailing overlapping layers across every possible entry point. So far, it had kept out the monsters, but the light always found a way in.

Before opening the door, he placed a small device in his ear and turned the tiny dial until it clicked. The sound of the boy's room filled his ear, the owl's heartbeat continuing to pulse. He hated going outside while his son slept, but it was safer to get some distance. Every night, the darkness found him. There was nothing he could do about that.

His right hand went about the work of undoing several locks on the door. His left hand grazed the hilt of his sword, feeling the worn leather that wrapped its ridges. The blade had once glowed brilliantly enough to light up the night, burning with a power he would have never believed had he not witnessed it himself. Years before, he thought he would use the weapon to wipe the scourge from the earth, to root out demons in the darkest places. He had been fearless then, and probably stupid.

But that was years ago.

Now, as he stepped across the threshold and scanned the grassy hills before him, he only hoped that his blade would not break this night.

Despite the lack of cover, he walked upright and at a brisk pace. Every so often, he glanced over his shoulder at the house. Somewhere in the distance behind it, his wife rested beneath a blanket of wildflowers. Memories of her touch brought love and anger, joy and pain, all swirling together like dark clouds in his mind. *It should have been her who survived.*

After cresting the largest hill, he dared for an instant to stare at the moon and dream that one day this would all end, that he could catch fireflies with his son under the evening sky without watching the horizon for danger.

But when the warrior lowered his gaze, he saw them coming.

The Wretched poured over the grass like a pestilence. They all mostly resembled each other; evil had an unsettling uniformity. Skin sagged and melted off their skulls. Black eyes glistened like onyx. They wore tattered clothes covered with dirt and dry blood. A few showed hints of scales under rotting, human flesh — the next signs of their dark evolution.

They came at him fast, their pace quickening at the sight of their prey. The warrior paused. Perhaps tonight, he would not lift his sword at all. He was tired of fighting an unwinnable war, tired of having any glimmer of hope snuffed out like a candle in a storm. The warrior could not defeat the dark forces any more than he could push away the night. He no longer feared death for his own sake.

But he had a son.

And so he drew his weapon.

The thin, rusty blade pulsed with a faint, blue energy that disappeared the moment it was unsheathed, then reappeared a few agonizing seconds later, though weaker than before. The creatures screamed as they reached him.

His movements were automatic. The first to attack were always the weakest. There was nothing these cursed pawns could do that he hadn't seen countless times. He ducked their clumsy swipes and sidestepped their charges, his sword carving lines into their decaying skin at exactly the right places. Once, the blade would have cut through the Wretched as if they were shadows. Time and repetition had dulled its edge, requiring more of his strength to defeat his attackers. *So much for promises and prophecy.*

But the warrior's movements were flawless, an economy of motion perfected over years of fighting. His feet never moved an inch farther than needed. His sword made no extra cuts. The Wretched fought with wild bloodlust and endless ferocity, but in minutes, they all lay crumpled at his feet.

The warrior held his head low. A cool wind pushed over his face as he mourned the bodies around him and prayed he wouldn't join them before his son was old enough to defend himself.

He searched the hills for signs of more. Could it possibly be over that quickly? His mind held no delusions of ultimate victory, but maybe tonight would provide some respite. He leaned back a little and prepared to take his first step toward the house, already warmed by thoughts of the sleeping bag he would roll out on his son's floor.

He should have known better.

The ground rumbled beneath him. His eyes darted across the broken landscape. It felt like the approach of a large vehicle. Maybe the Wretched were few tonight because there were military units in the area. That didn't necessarily mean safety; the world was not as it once had been. But at least other humans weren't drawn to him in the same way. With a bit of luck, they would pass him by.

Unfortunately, there were no vehicles in sight.

The rumble continued, sending tremors up the warrior's aching body. He looked down and saw the earth crack under his feet.

He danced back as the ground ripped apart with a muffled roar. The first thing he saw were the horns—long, black, and twisted—atop a head of dark scales. The lines between the scales glowed red as if hot coals blazed beneath the surface. A massive arm appeared and pushed down against the ground, lifting a fiery-eyed demon from the depths.

When it had fully emerged, the hulking brute blotted out the moonlight. This was no Wretched, but it served the same master.

Then this is how it ends. The warrior took a readied position, though in his heart, he saw no path to survival.

The sword vibrated in his hand. He looked down to see its glow flicker, then die.

His eyes were still on the blade when the demon hammered him with a fist the size of a boulder. His body went numb and his mind darkened as the blow sent him tumbling across the grass.

When he finally stopped skidding, blood and dirt filled his mouth. Every inch of him burned with pain, but somehow he had managed to hold on to the dead sword.

The ground trembled as the beast charged.

The warrior's head swam. Black fog crept around the edges of his vision, but he stumbled to his feet and managed to dodge the next attack.

He swung his sword, the lifeless blade clanging harmlessly off the monster's flesh. In years past, many demons had fallen to the weapon.

At least, he *thought* they had. His sanity and salvation were mere assumptions at this point.

The beast attacked again, and the warrior countered with a desperate slash. The demon knocked the blade aside and sliced his left shoulder with its claws. He hardly had time to recognize the pain before a second strike caught him in the face.

His body spun through the air. The sword flew from his gasp.

He slammed into the ground, his face in the dirt.

A low growl and thunderous steps filled the night as the demon approached, savoring the moment before the kill, perhaps disgusted that its enemy hadn't offered a more satisfying battle.

The warrior could feel the beast behind him, but he kept his head down. Blood pooled in the grass beneath his shoulder. Pain racked his body, but he could move. He had been hurt worse many times before.

So many times. The pain felt distant somehow, but the weariness engulfed him. Even if he defeated this demon, there would be another. If not tomorrow, then the day after, and all the days forever until he could fight no more.

The pain swelled again. Blood seeped out of his body in time with his beating heart, which grew louder in his ears each moment.

Then, it stopped.

His breath caught, and he realized it hadn't been his own heart that stopped, but the sound created by an owl-shaped machine that transmitted to the device in his ear. It had been with him the entire time, but he hadn't noticed it until it ceased. Fear filled the silence—terror worse than pain. What had happened to his son?

And then, the sound returned, accompanied by a whisper of love and innocence in the darkness.

"Dada."

The warrior rolled away an instant before the demon's claws ripped into the ground where his head had been. His own life may be forever cursed by the sins of his past, but he would *not* die lying down, not when his son still needed him.

The warrior dove for the sword, the weapon he had carried on his journey from ignorance to faith, from faith to anger, from anger to despair. He would carry it again into death.

But by God, he would not die alone.

The instant his fingers wrapped around the hilt, the blade flared to life, vivid blue energy racing down the length of the blade like the power of stars painted over steel.

The warrior whirled as the demon leapt into the air with fangs bared and claws outstretched, but he recognized fear in the depths of those black eyes. A glimmer of blue reflected in them as well.

He raised the sword.

For my son.

The blade did the rest, piercing the demon's skin as if carving through water.

The monster bellowed as it hit the ground. The warrior came to a knee, ready to press the attack.

The intensity of the flames between the demon's scales grew as if consuming the creature from the inside. It tried to roar again, but the sound was choked by its own crumbling flesh. The warrior watched as jaws of fire devoured its own.

Seconds later, a strong wind blew across the valley, carrying the beast's ashes into the darkness.

The warrior stood, sheathed his sword, and waited. The demon was gone, and *he* was alive.

The horizon stood empty. The earth, quiet. No more Wretched would come this night, and so, the warrior stumbled back toward the house, his thoughts already drifting to his next inevitable battle. When he was younger, destroying a demon would have brought visions of a day when there would be no more Wretched, no more monsters, no more madness. He would be the hero he'd always imagined.

Now, he knew differently. Lying to himself would only make him more vulnerable when reality ripped away his paper world and left his soul in tatters. Truth was a better strategy, and his child was all the motivation he needed. Winning the war might not mean conquering the dark enemy, but keeping it at bay for another night. He may never defeat it, but that did not mean it would never be defeated.

For now, he fought so his son could see the light of one more day.
And that was enough.

SPIRIT OF THE JAGUAR
Cassandra Hamm

He isn't coming back. I've been watching the rainforest's border all day, waiting for Edgardo, flanked by the dark jaguar, to stride through the smattering of mud huts and announce that our people are free. But it's sundown, and my clenching gut tells me that yet another man is lost.

Sweat dripping down my cheeks, I kick dirt over the smoldering coals, pull down the rest of the washing, and march inside. I won't continue my foolish lookout any longer. Every second hurts more. Another one of my people dead.

Setting her tray on the table, Mamá moves to kiss my cheeks. In her dark eyes is an unspoken question I'm not quite ready to answer.

"The empanadas smell *delicioso*, Mamá." I breathe in deeply, the scent of freshly baked dough filling my nostrils. But even that is not enough to untangle the knots in my stomach.

Mamá's smile bunches the wrinkles on her brown skin. "Gracias, Jesenia."

I set the washing on the table and begin to fold, the movements familiar and calming. Anything to stop me from thinking about Edgardo's flesh in Ambrosio's stomach, his bones littering the rainforest floor. The sweltering heat wraps me in an unwanted blanket.

Finally, the question comes. "What of Edgardo?"

My hands still. After a moment, I say, "He hasn't returned."

Mamá turns away, her eyes cast toward the dirt floor. "Poor Carmen. She should not be a widow so young."

A shriek splits the air--no doubt Carmen finally accepting that her husband has perished. The wailing tears into my soul. How can the gods do this to us? Their ambassadors are here to protect us, not devour us, yet they refuse to defend us against the invaders!

Leaning on his crutch, Desi limps into the kitchen. I force

my mind away from Edgardo's bloody fate and smile at my brother.

"There you are!" I kiss his forehead, hoping to ease some of the pain from his eyes. "Have you been staying out of trouble?"

His grin is forced. "No."

I ruffle his thick hair, already spiked from the humidity. "I should've known."

He pushes away from me. "Are the empanadas ready yet?"

"Sí, you impatient scoundrel." Mamá mock-scowls at him. "Now, I'll let you help me set them out, but *only* if you don't sneak one while you think I'm not watching."

Giggling, he begins his unsteady walk, cane thumping. "You're always watching, Mamá."

"That's right," she says. "And don't you forget it, *mijo*."

When Desi has left, I say, "You're upset."

"Of course." She averts her gaze. Carmen's cries fill the silence. "A man has died."

"Mamá." I fold my arms over my chest.

Her face crumples like kneaded dough. "It is tomorrow, Jesenia," she whispers. "He will be sent out tomorrow."

The breath leaves my lungs. The elders will send my crippled brother into the rainforest to face death at the hands of a vengeful spirit. How *could* they? "You can't let him go, Mamá."

"It is our family's turn next." Her voice cracks. "We must send someone."

"How about *me?*" My blood is hot beneath my skin. "Papá taught me to fight."

Mamá's eyes harden. "Only men can seek the spirit. You know that."

I stalk back to the washing, my heartbeat thumping in my ears. Desi has enough difficulty walking around the village, crutch in hand, tripping on the uneven ground. How can the elders expect him to navigate the *rainforest?*

Even if Desi finds Ambrosio, who's to say that he will be able to bond with the head spirit? The elders say there will be some sort of mark on the ambassador that links the two minds, but we don't even know that for sure. Besides, judging by our eight missing tribesmen, Ambrosio is not eager to bond. And what if he looks poorly on the lame? Desi won't stand a chance.

I hardly notice the scent of fruity empanadas and Desi's chirping, "Time to eat!"

How can he be so cheerful? Surely he knows why he is being spoiled tonight. Unless…

I freeze. Looking at Mamá, I mouth, "Does he know?"

She looks away. That's all the answer I need. I'm about to erupt when a familiar voice interrupts me.

"Jesenia?"

I whip my face toward the open door, which frames the willowy figure of my cousin Maristela.

"Mari! Good to see you." Mamá kisses Maristela's cheeks. "Did you eat?"

"Sí, *Tía* Iolanda." Maristela's teeth gleam in a blinding smile. "Papá says I can stay the night if that's all right with you."

"Of course!" Mamá gestures toward the table. "Please, have an empanada. Desi, another plate."

He limps away.

Maristela takes my hands in hers and kisses my cheeks. Her dark eyes search mine, and I see the same sadness reflected there--the same sorrow for our people.

If only the invaders had never come. Now they bear down on us with their weapons and horses, seeking concubines and slaves. The cripples, useless in their eyes, they would execute. I have heard horrific tales passed from other villages of their cruelty.

Not that it matters. Desi will die tomorrow, anyway.

My fists tighten around hers, and she frowns a little. I shake my head.

We sit at the table, and I force myself to make light conversation. Thunder rumbles outside, promising torrents. The empanada tastes like ash in my mouth. All I can do is stare at my brother's sweet face and imagine what our home will be like without him. First Papá, now *mi hermano*. Soon Mamá, Maristela, and I will be concubines to foreign men.

My jaw tightens. I won't let that happen. Tonight, either I'll die, or my people will be free.

৵৵৵

The rainforest has proven its name this evening. Rain pounds against the leaves at the top of the canopy and plummets to the floor far beneath. I yank my boot from the mud with a sucking noise and make my way toward a lluvia tree. Heat thickens the air, mingling with the raindrops.

I wipe at the water dripping into my eyes and run my fingers along a deep gash in the bark--a claw mark.

"We're in Ambrosio's territory now," I say.

Maristela squishes her way toward me and interlocks our shaking fingers. "Be kind to him," she says.

Kind? To a spirit who is killing my people, both with his claws and with his inaction? Scoffing, I peer at the canopy far above and wonder if Ambrosio is hiding among the upper branches. I can almost hear Papá whispering in my ear, "Careful, *mija*. Stay alert. The rainforest holds many secrets."

"Ambrosio won't listen to you if you shout."

"What else am I supposed to do? Ask him politely?"

"*Tío* Alvaro would have been kind."

Blinking rapidly, I stare at the leafy floor. She is right. Papá *would* be kind. But I'm not him.

"I'll try," I say, and Maristela smiles. "*But,* if he doesn't listen, I will fight."

Her smile fades. "If you must."

I squeeze Maristela's wet hand. The pressure of her palm against mine stifles at least some of the panic, but the noises of the forest--cawing, croaking, hissing, chirping, and the *rain*--leaves me deaf to all but the memory of Papá's voice: "Remember what I taught you, mija."

He should be the one traversing this rainforest. People always took his advice; perhaps a great spirit would have done the same.

"Your braid is coming undone." Maristela reaches for the hair clinging to my neck, but I shrug away her hand. "Let me fix it."

"It's raining, Mari. My hair is destined to be a mess." I peer through the thick foliage for a hint of black fur. Perhaps Ambrosio doesn't expect me to be a petitioner since I'm a girl. Perhaps that is why he hides his fearsome face.

What will happen when we find him? What will happen if I *fail?* Perhaps Maristela will manage to escape. But would death be better than the fate of a concubine?

I shake the thoughts away. I won't fail. I can't afford to.
But will kindness truly sway him, as Mari believes?
"Ambrosio? I have come to speak with you," I say.
Maristela grips my shoulder. "Don't hurt him, Jesenia. Please."
If only I could hurt him…
The ferns rustle as something emerges from the darkness. Ambrosio stands before me, his sopping fur darker than the night sky, his eyes glowing like moons, his limbs lithe and powerful. Long, pointed teeth hook over his black lips, and I swallow hard.
"Yet another human who's come to beg." Ambrosio's growl is rich and deep, almost melodic. Despite my mental preparation, seeing words come from the jaguar's gaping jaws still leaves me unbalanced. "Your people must be desperate if they are sending a woman."
"They didn't send me." I straighten my shoulders. "I came of my own will."
"Foolish girl."
I blink away the raindrops, trying to ignore the insult's sting.
Ambrosio's tail flicks from side to side. "You know that in speaking to me, if you fail to convince me of the merits of your request, you will have chosen death."
The image of Desi hobbling into the woods burns into my mind. "I know." I won't make him come before this terrifying spirit. I *can't* fail.
"So, what have you come to offer me, human? Useless trinkets? Power of which I have no need?"
I flinch.
"*Lo siento.*" Maristela's quavering apology is barely audible over the rain's drumbeat. "We--"
"Enough of your chatter." Ambrosio shakes his head from side to side, flinging raindrops. "Who is the leader here?"
"I… I am." I take a step forward, sloshing in the mud. "I'm Jesenia. I've come because--"
"Your village is about to be destroyed. I'm well aware."
My mouth snaps shut.
"Is that all?" His massive jaws gape in a yawn.

Heat tinges my cheeks. "Don't you care?"

"No."

"You *should*." My hands shake with rage. "They'll come after *you* next. They don't like forests, don't like spirits. They'll destroy everything you hold dear."

"They can try." He flicks his tail. "You humans believe too much in your own futile power."

My chest heaves up and down. The most powerful of the forest spirits isn't supposed to be a cynical creature incapable of caring for anyone but himself.

Maristela grabs my arm. "Let me talk to him," she says. "Perhaps I can—"

I shoulder her aside and glare at Ambrosio. "My brother is coming here tomorrow." Hot tears streak down my cheeks, mingling with the raindrops. "My sweet, crippled hermano will *die* begging you unless you help us now."

"You speak as if death is a surprise. Why can't mortals understand the inevitability of the end?"

I clench my jaw. If he won't allow me to bond with him, then I will make him.

"*Prima*, no!" Maristela cries as I leap at the jaguar.

My feet slip in the mud, and I land awkwardly, unbalanced. He knocks me over with a paw, but I drag myself from the mud and attack again, this time landing on his back. I try to lock my arms around his neck, but he throws me off as if I am nothing.

I stand, legs burning, mud-smeared. Only his pale eyes distinguish him from the darkness. He prowls a moment longer, then pounces. I dive away, Maristela's screams echoing in my ears, and almost slam my head against a tree. Shoving myself to my feet, I launch onto his back once more, this time successfully clinging to his neck. Yowling, he bucks, and my slick hands slip. I hit the ground, wheezing. His claws score down my back. I scream, my breath coming hot and fast.

"Please don't fight!" Maristela wails.

I roll away from Ambrosio, yelping as mud smears on my wound, and stand. Something akin to boredom shines in his yellow eyes. I wipe the rain from my forehead and tuck my hair behind my ear. I should've let Maristela fix the braid.

I search Ambrosio's fur for a mark—something, *anything*. If I don't find it, I'll face the same fate as the eight men before me.

"Ambrosio, please, just *help* us!" Maristela cries. "It doesn't have to end like this."

Ambrosio leaps. I dive beneath him and roll into a standing position, my back screaming. I again scan his fur for imperfections, but he pins me before I can react. My head slams against the mud, and I moan, pain radiating through my body. But there, on the underside of his neck, the fur has been burned away to reveal a faint spiral.

"Your end would have come, anyway." Ambrosio's breath is hot on my face, his jaws dripping with saliva. "If you humans don't kill each other, your own body does. You are destined for destruction."

His heavy body presses against mine, restraining my hands. I'm so close! I just need to touch the spiral… His claws dig into my arms with each jerk.

"But now, this will be the last pain you will ever feel. Trust me, human, I am doing you a favor."

I convulse beneath him in a wild effort to free my hands. I can do it. I can save my people--

I hear thumping footsteps, see a brown blur.

"No!" Maristela's cry splits the air as she throws her slender arms around Ambrosio's neck, squeezing. Her hand brushes against the spiral.

Ambrosio's fearsome jaws close, and he gazes around as if it's his first time among the trees. Maristela's eyes shine like the moon, and her skin emits a faint glow. My mouth drops.

"I… I can feel him," she whispers. "His heartbeat. The pressure of his mind."

Dear gods above. Maristela has bonded with Ambrosio. My sweet prima will be our deliverer.

Ambrosio stands, and I struggle to my feet. My head throbs, and my back stings like his claws are piercing it again and again. But I can't stop staring at my cousin and the great spirit.

His eyes lock with hers, unspoken communication passing between them. Blood drips from my back, and I blink, rain tracing the contours of my face.

"You truly love your people," Ambrosio says at last. "I have never felt the strength of such love before."

"Please don't let them die." Tears well in Maristela's eyes. "You are our only hope, Ambrosio. Kill me if you must, but save my people."

Rain pounds against the ground for several long moments. Then Ambrosio roars, but I'm not afraid — this roar is a cry against the injustice our people face. We're saved. *Desi* is saved!

I slump. "You have saved us all."

"No." Maristela wraps her arms around me, squeezing tightly. "*We* have saved us all."

THE STORMS OF POSEIDON
Patrick M. Fitzgerald

Zach grinned when he saw Poseidon enter the Pegasus's view screen. It was registered as an M-class planet, but that hadn't necessarily meant it would look like Earth. The land mass seemed smaller, and the weather patterns were a bit more turbulent, but otherwise it closely resembled the mother world. And even for a native of the Titan colony like Zach, its "classic" appearance still tugged at his heartstrings.

Looking down at the spaceport city from his view screen, his eyes followed the nearby sprawling coastline then the blue-green forests that made up most of the land in the area. Its nostalgic beauty almost made him forget that he was here on a peacekeeping mission with alien natives. Almost.

After docking and shuffling through the arrival procedures, Zach made his way to the Welcome Station's lounge where Kay waited. The area was decorated with odd, woven domes, the layers of which rotated slowly in the fans' breeze. It was less crowded than Zach had expected, and his sister's rich auburn hair and orange sunglasses made her immediately recognizable. She perched on a nearby barstool with a glass of iced tea, reviewing data on her wrist-computer.

"Heya, sis. Good to see you again," Zach said with a grin as he swung himself onto the next stool. He tossed his knapsack onto the bar and elbowed his sister. "Been a while, eh?"

A smile crept onto her face as she nudged him back without looking up. "Yeah, I'm glad I had the excuse to see you again." She glanced up shyly and nodded to him. She'd grown a bit since he'd last seen her, and she sat with more poise and confidence than he remembered.

"Hah. I *thought* it sounded like something you could handle by yourself." He grinned wider.

"Oh, I assure you, I couldn't have. The tritons really, *really* don't trust the colonists here. I may just have been the translator, but they insisted on dealing only with me when they found out I was an offworlder."

Zach's eyebrows shot up. "You're kidding? So you're conducting the entire negotiations for the colonists?"

She grimaced. "Yeah, but I don't know anything about tech-trade laws."

Zach shrugged dismissively. "Not much to know, really. It's just the high-end stuff that the Planetary Coalition wants to keep to itself: Interstellar travel, nuclear power, genetic engineering. Basically the stuff that could cause a society to collapse if they got it too soon."

Kay took off her sunglasses and tapped them against her glass. "Yeah, that's the problem. They want interstellar travel."

Zach winced. "That *is* a problem. What are they like?"

"Their language is beautiful, lyric and tonal." She gazed off for a moment in reflection. "Physically, they're sort of spidery, toothpick-thin, and have joints everywhere. They're also ridiculously tall, too much so for clearance on a standard passenger ship. But they're really nice once you get to know them." She shrugged, then glanced around the lounge. "Most people here don't."

Zach shook his head. "It's never good when neighbors don't trust each other." He scanned the room and noticed a sculpture in the corner. "Is that native art?" It seemed to be made of plant fibers, woven into a chaotic spider-web design with no discernible repeating pattern, and shaped into a hemispherical dome adorned with three polished disks. Some of the fibers were a natural, dark blue-green, some were bleached white, and the rest had been dyed a rich sapphire. He had to tip his sunglasses up to fully appreciate the colors, and having grown up in an orange atmosphere, the bright, almost mystical shades of blue left a tingling sensation on his retinas.

"Yeah. Most of their art looks something like that. General opinion is that it's probably meant to be abstract." She tilted up her own sunglasses.

"Think it's a globe?" he mused.

"It reminds me more of a dream catcher, so I'm guessing it has a similar spiritual significance."

Something about it bugged him. It had no symmetry at all,

which was extremely difficult to achieve by accident. Things usually fell into patterns naturally.

Kay cleared her throat. "The tritons insist that we meet with them tomorrow in West Port. The colonial government wants us to wait until the storms pass, but there's no telling when that'll happen."

Zach chuckled and quaffed the last of his drink. "With everything humanity's been able to achieve, you'd think we could tell when it's going to rain."

ೂೂೂ

Rainfall drummed on the roof of the hovercraft as Zach and Kay arrived at the shore of West Port.

The native buildings, arranged in a circle, were fragile constructs of long, pliable branches woven together into domes. Three tritons waited in the middle of the circle, seemingly unconcerned by the downpour.

As Kay had said, they were enormous, at least three meters tall even hunched over as they were. They rested on the back four of their eight legs, which seemed to sink into the ground, and held the front pairs aloft, waving them rhythmically in the pelting rain.

"Zach, I'd like you to meet Teesha, liaison of the Triton Nation. This is Eullee, her translator, and Orrin, the secretary. Honored representatives, this is my brother, Zach Karr."

They each extended a forelimb in greeting, and Zach made an attempt to greet them, but each of their limbs terminated in a sharp, bony spike that made shaking hands difficult.

"It is a pleasure to meet you, my new friends," Zach said with a deep bow. Considering their massive size, it was a meaningless gesture, but he needed to get the rain off his face for a moment.

"We welcome you, Zach Karr," Eullee intoned in a deeply resonant voice, drawing out each vowel as she spoke. Her accent minimized gutturals, so his name sounded more like "Zaa... Arr." "I speak for Teesha, who speaks for our people." Teesha tilted her cylindrical body slightly and hummed a brief response.

"You can call me Z," he said.

"Zee..." the three natives intoned. They drew the syllable out as they rubbed their forelimbs together, as though caressing the sound.

"We find Poseidon's mood most interesting now." Eullee said. "We must share with him now, before the time for business."

"I hope that by sharing this with you I shall... understand." Zach's response received an approving nod from his sister.

The three tritons lowered their bodies to his level, giving him his first good view of their faces, the only distinguishing feature of which was a bluish bulge in the front; given that it was semi-transparent and reflective, it was likely the eye.

"We hope you will understand," Eullee said slowly. "Will you sing with us?"

Realizing how quickly he'd achieved this breakthrough, Zach gave a lopsided grin and wink to his sister. Her eyes were wide with surprise.

Teesha intoned a single, rising note, which her two associates joined in turn. The tone continued, shifting rapidly in pitch with no pause for the intake of breath. A simple melody presented itself — Orrin's slightly lower voice harmonized directly with Teesha's while Eullee's wove in and out as an exotic counterpoint.

Zach added his baritone voice awkwardly to the song and managed to give it a more rhythmic texture. Kay began to intone along with Teesha, her ear for music being as flawless as her ear for language.

The four of them worked deeper and deeper into the song, improvising an ever-changing melody in response to the rain and wind blowing through the willowy trees. They grew louder to match the escalating storm's howling wind, and Zach was sure that they had been singing for hours when a red light began blinking furiously on Kay's wrist unit.

Her face blanched, and she leaned in closer to Zach. "We need to take shelter. *Now.*"

The natives looked completely undeterred. It crossed Zach's mind that perhaps the aliens had become too distracted to notice the weather, but their song matched it too perfectly.

Orrin watched Zach and Kay closely and spoke in his own language to his companions. Eullee leaned close to Zach and intoned, "You are as an infant?"

This isn't the time to exchange insults. Frowning, Zach made eye contact with his sister, who nodded, though a smile twitched at the corner of her mouth.

Against the unrelenting storm, Zach couldn't deny the appropriateness of the term. "Yes. At the moment, I am."

The three natives conferred amongst themselves and seemed to come to a quick resolution. "Then we shall be as parents."

Eullee slipped the spike of one forelimb under Zach's arms, letting him grasp tightly, then arched him backwards under her body. Teesha pulled his sister up in the same way. Eullee's membranous underbelly flaps withdrew much the way the petals of a rose open, revealing delicate skin beneath. Zach's heart raced as he fought the sudden urge to flee, to twist away and face the storm alone, but, as Eullee said, he was as a child, and the membranes enveloped him firmly despite his reservations, holding him in place.

He panicked for a moment and assumed imminent suffocation, but each breath, though humid and a bit musty, came as easily as the last. And so, he sighed and squinted through the membrane across his face, watching sheets of water crash through the natives' shelters, leaving broken shards of wood in their wake. Eullee swayed with the wind, but his multi-jointed legs seemed to absorb the energy without difficulty

Chunks of what Zach could only guess were the remains of the colonists' buildings flew by periodically, a few coming perilously close and eliciting agile evasions from the natives. Multiple times he saw the bodies of people who had either not had time to evacuate or, more likely, had underestimated the ultimate severity of the storm. He squeezed his eyes closed after a while, unable to bear the sight any longer, and tears welled up within them.

The aftermath would be just as bad as the storm itself. The surviving colonists would feel betrayed. The aliens had probably known its severity but had anticipated it with awe rather than fear. Their response seemed built into their very physiology.

"Eullee, how long will this continue?" Zach's voice came out muffled, but Eullee responded through the membranes nonetheless.

"Until Poseidon's mood subsides."

Zach sighed, closing his eyes again. For now, his life was in her hands.

§~§~§

Zach couldn't be sure how long the storm had lasted—he thought he might have fallen asleep at some point—but he startled when the membranes started to finally unwrap from around him. They unfolded as a flower opening itself into the sunlight, unveiling the deluged world. A glittering rainbow arched across a third of the sky like Saturn's rings embracing the wreckage of West Port. Zach blinked several times, and he reflexively slipped on his sunglasses.

The tips of Eullee's forelimbs slipped under his arms, and he gripped them as they lowered him back to the ground. His feet sank into the mud like the legs of the natives, anchoring them despite being wobbly after hours of confinement and disuse.

"You understand now," Eullee said, her iridescent eye gazing at him. "You are one of the tritons."

"I'm honored, dear friends, and I thank you for your protection." Zach pressed a hand to Eullee's forelimb. "It's a shame the colonists here don't see you as I do."

The three natives conferred for a moment, and Eullee turned back to him. "We still seek access to interstellar travel. Do you have the authority to grant it to us?"

"I have the authority." More specifically, he was authorized by the Coalition to give them anything that would dissuade them from gaining access to four-space technology. Close enough. "I do not have reason to do so, though."

The aliens exchanged a look. "But, that is the technology we desire in exchange for the rental of the land."

"Zach made a wide gesture to the devastated city. "The treaty clearly states that you are to provide all information you have about the land. This obviously includes storms of this magnitude. As deeply compassionate as you are, I don't understand why you didn't provide a warning."

Eullee glanced at her companions. They stood in silence as Orrin began swirling his forelimbs in the mud. "But we did," Eullee intoned slowly.

Zach was stunned, but he knew that they couldn't have. The

colonists would have evacuated the city sooner if they'd known.

"We provided numerous copies of the Poseidon Codex. Much effort went into ensuring that each was flawless in design." Eullee pointed with a few limbs at the design Orrin had made.

Zach stared at it, trying to discern exactly what it was that Orrin had depicted. Something felt familiar about it, something in the chaotic—

Of course. It was the same non-repeating pattern woven into the sculpture back at the lounge. The revelation swelled into despair in Zach's gut.

"They... didn't understand," he said weakly. That was the purpose of the sculpture. It wasn't artwork at all, but an intricately crafted diagram of the weather patterns on the planet.

The three natives began emitting a high-pitched whine. Eullee said, "They claimed that they understood."

Zach shook his head in frustration at the colonists' carelessness. "They didn't even *understand* what they didn't understand."

The whine dropped in pitch, a clear sound of pity.

Zach's statement flickered into an idea—a glimmer of hope. "And you see, that's how it is with interstellar travel."

The three natives turned their eyes to each other in silence, and then they turned back to him. "We do not understand what would need to be understood," Eullee said, deeply pensive. "Will you promise to yield it to us when we do understand?"

"Yes. I will."

"We trust you as one of us and accept your promise. The treaty is upheld."

ೞೞೞ

"I don't know how you do it, Z," Kay said, drying her hair in their room at the spaceport lounge.

"It wasn't anything remarkable. I was just nice to them."

"Well, it'll fetch a hefty chunk of credit considering that you got away with a handshake and a promise."

"More than that, Kay." Zach adjusted the triton's sculpture, repositioning the wooden disks until they aligned with the positions of the planet's moons. As he slid them backwards, the patterns on the dome shifted to show the storm they had just experienced.

"But, you know the Coalition will never give them access to the tech."

He turned back to her, a wry grin tilting his lips. "I told them I'd give it to them when they understood it. And I will. I'll give them the drive from the Pegasus if I have to."

"Zach, you can't—."

Zach shrugged. "I'll do what I must to keep my promise, and to keep the peace."

THE REVEALING
E.S. Marsh

I stop picking at the single chin hair I've managed to grow in my sixteen years. "Ma, you're staring again."

My mother drops the burlap window flap like a hot coal. "Well the village is starting to gather, and there's still so much to do."

That's a load of dragon dung. I couldn't sleep last night, so I finished all my chores before dawn. By the time I came back inside, Ma had food sacks prepared for all four of us. Since then, she's just been sweeping an already spotless floor and announcing every time another family makes their way to Watcher's Hill.

"Ma, no one is ever early for their own Revealing."

"Please, Alvero. Just tell me if we're going to need one meal or two."

I pick at my nails. "I'm... not supposed to say."

"You don't have to tell me what you're going to reveal. Just how long it's going to take to reveal it." I open my mouth to tell her my secret, but she's peeking out the window again. "There goes Hayden," she says. "His Revealing took a week, remember? A week!"

"That dotard tamed a wild horse for his Revealing. Of course it took forever."

Ma grabs the broom and shakes it at me. "Young man, I didn't raise you to insult good, hard-working people. You watch. Master Darian will bring Hayden on as apprentice any day now."

"Not if he can't outsmart his horses."

"What was that?"

"Nothing," I say. Then add "ma'am" for good measure.

To be honest, I like Hayden. He'd make a great stable master. It's just I've been dying to talk to someone about this whole Revealing thing, but it's not allowed. I guess that's making me a bit of a grump. It's not that I don't want to become a man. I do. I want to display my worth to the elders. I want to be assigned a job so I can contribute to the village and the greater good, blah, blah, blah.

But the problem is, I'm not *good* at anything. Not for lack of trying. I'm okay at letters and figures. I can milk the cow without her kicking. Sometimes I help Ma with cooking or Pa with chopping wood. I even made a dress for my sister's smelly old doll. I can do those things, but I don't do them well. I still count on my fingers, I burn the bottom of the porridge every time, and the dress ended up shorter on one side.

I feel a tug on my tunic.

My sister's clutching her doll. "Can I help at your Revealing?"

I try not to smile, but I'm not good at that either. "No, Talia. That would be breaking the rules. You know what would happen."

"I won't tell."

I give her nose a pinch. "I would be honored to have your help, but I don't feel like being lunch for the dragon today."

"When do *I* get to have a Revealing?"

I pause. Girls don't have Revealings. I look at Ma, who gives me her don't-you-say-anything look.

Ma spins Talia around. "Honey, why don't you find Dolly's prettiest dress? She should look her finest on your brother's special day."

Talia smiles. Which means we all smile. She practically flies up the stairs. Ma sighs and picks the broom up again.

"It's not fair." I know. Not a very manly response, but I can't help it.

"She'll understand when she's older," says Ma, but I wasn't talking about Talia. I want to tell Ma my secret: I have nothing to reveal. I'd give anything for her advice, but people who speak of their Revealing get sent to the dragon. And those sent to the dragon either come back mad or not at all.

The door opens, and Pa's big, hairy frame ducks inside. "Alvero, it's time."

My heart feels like it's trying to escape through my throat. Fear must show on my face because Pa tugs me into one of his spine-cracking hugs.

"It doesn't matter how your Revealing goes, son. I'm already proud of you."

I mumble a reply. Pa slaps me on the back so hard that I tumble out the door. Right as the smith and his family walk by. His twin daughters giggle, whispering to each other as they pass. I wince at the heat flaring in my cheeks.

This is it. I'm out of time. Wings and whiskers, what am I going to do? I'll have to admit in front of the entire village that I'm nothing. A failure. They'll give me to the dragon for sure.

I don't remember walking to the fields. We're just suddenly there. Ma, Pa, and Talia are sitting at the foot of Watcher's Hill. Ma nods to the platform constructed at its base. I blink away the stupid tears forming in my eyes.

There's giggling from farther up. Probably the twins, curse them. I shuffle to the platform and sag under the stares of the people I've grown up with, the village I'm about to let down.

Elder Borin stands and raises a wobbling hand. The people hush. I force myself to keep breathing because my body doesn't want to on its own anymore.

"Alvero, son of Elvaro, do you embrace your community and give your best for the benefit of all?"

Mediocracy may be the best I can offer, but I nod. Elder Borin raises a bushy eyebrow.

I clear my throat, but my voice still cracks when I say, "Aye."

More accursed, girlish laughter.

"Villagers of Hilltop, do you accept this man into the community and vow to support his family, should the earth take him before his prime?"

A robust round of affirmation from the menfolk follow a chorus of ayes.

Elder Borin sits among his peers. "Alvero, son of Elvaro, what do you reveal?"

I grip my tunic to keep my hands from shaking. "I... um..." Come on, think, think, *think!* Gods above and below, I wish I could reveal an ability to disappear. Someone coughs. My parents exchange a look. I have to say something. Anything!

"For my Revealing I... I will slay the dragon."

My eyes widen as the words leave my mouth. Villagers

gasp. Pa looks pale. The elders huddle together in quiet conversation. Shouldn't everyone be relieved? If there were no dragon, there would be nothing to fear about becoming a man.

I don't know how, but time skips ahead again. The crowd is gone. Ma gives me a squeeze. My hair is wet from her tears. A small pile of mismatched armor and a sword lay at my feet. I scoop it up as Hayden points up Watcher's Hill toward the caves. I guess someone has to witness the deed. Otherwise, I might run off. Suddenly, I'm certain that's exactly what happened to some of the men that never returned from the dragon's cave. They ran…

The temptation lasts only a moment. I may not be gifted, but I'm no coward, either. Fool that I am, I will meet the fate I chose.

The armor is heavier than it looks. My undershirt is sticky with sweat before we're halfway there. Despite my slogged pace, we arrive before sun fall. The cave is shaped almost like the mouth of a dragon. I peer into the dark, stone throat. Hayden drops his gear and digs a pit for the fire.

"You coming?" I ask.

Hayden shrugs. "I'm good with animals. If you want, I'll go."

I almost say yes, but I can tell he doesn't like the look of the ominous entrance any more than I do. His face relaxes some when I say I should continue alone.

I take my first steps inside. The cave isn't as cold as I expect it to be, and I'm sweating through the chain shirt. I take off the helmet so I can see better in the gloom. Just when I fear that the crevasse I'm scooting through doesn't actually lead anywhere, it spits me out into a narrow but tall cavern. Rocks lie in a heap on the other side. I start forward, but my sword wedges between the two walls of the tunnel. The more I pull, the more stuck it gets.

"What, pray tell, do you hope to accomplish with *that*?"

I jump so hard that I bump my head. Should have kept the helmet on. "Is… someone there?"

"Answer the question."

It's a matronly voice that reminds me of Pa's mum when she was alive. But what would any sane person be doing in a dragon's cave on purpose? I duck under the sword and inch into the cavern. I don't see anyone, and there's not much to hide behind except those rocks. One of them shifts. Son of a salamander, someone must be stuck!

"Do you need help?" I ask.

The rocks quiver. A rumble echoes through the cavern. "I cannot comprehend a single task a human can do that a dragon cannot, but I am pleased that you offer. No one ever has."

Fear springs from my chest to my mind. Those aren't rocks. I'm within arm's reach of the dragon's belly. There's a choking noise like when our dog gets a bone caught in his throat. A pool of molten liquid splashes in front of me. From its light, I see a claw the size of a pony. I stumble back until I feel the wedged sword at my back.

"What do you see, man-boy?"

"You're... the dragon." I swallow. If I keep her talking, maybe she won't eat me. "I didn't expect you to sound so... fancy." Another rumble vibrates through the rock. Laughter. Without my permission, my body relaxes a bit.

"Most unusual."

"Is it?" I risk a step closer.

"Quite." After another choking sound, more lava drips into the glowing pool, revealing the dragon's long neck and wide head. Her eyes glow like embers.

"If the truth cannot be perceived by a man, then neither can he perceive me. But you evade my question. Why have you come?"

I wipe the sweat from my brow. "I have come to slay—"

The dragon lets out a fierce growl that vibrates my ribs. "It is a grave offense to deceive a dragon. Do not lie to me again."

I should be frightened, but my shoulders drop with relief. It's true. I never thought even for a moment that I could actually kill the dragon. But then why did I say I would? And in front of the whole village?

The dragon's eyes lower to my level. "Why do you seek me, man-boy?"

I think carefully before I answer. "I didn't know what else to do."

The dragon settles like a cat about to take a nap. "You seek enlightenment?"

Do I? "Today is my Revealing, but I have no skills. No

strengths. The elders would have sent me here, anyway."

The dragon purrs. "You think men are sent here as punishment?"

"Aren't they?"

Another chuckle rumbles through the rock floor. "No. Your wise ones know us dragons are truth weavers. They send men to me when truth is lost."

"What about when they don't come back?"

"Unfortunately, some men prefer death over truth. Which is what lying to a dragon is. I simply give them what they wish."

"And those who go mad?"

The dragon pauses, nibbling at the skin between her claws. "If you could see naught but my shadow or my words came only as whispers to you, would you not retreat into the safety of your own mind, nest of lies that it might be?"

I nod. I'll certainly not be so quick to judge the next time I see a mumbling mess of a man in the doorway of a tavern.

I don't know if I want to know the answer to my next question, but I ask it anyway. "Do any survive your truth weaving?"

The dragon looks at me for so long that I close my eyes and still see the glow of hers.

"Not many. It takes great bravery to hear, comprehend, and accept the truth."

I don't think I've lost my mind yet, so does that mean I'm brave? No one's ever called me that before.

I shed the rest of my armor. Without it, I feel lighter. Taller. The spark of a thought grows to a flame in my mind. "I thought you were a pile of rocks at first, but when you spoke, I saw you. And I've heard you clearly from the start." The dragon flicks a forked tongue in my direction as I continue. "There are things I know sometimes even though I shouldn't. Like when Grandmum found peace, I knew Pa cried, but only when no one else could see. Talia helped. My sister, she has a gift. She can make anyone smile. Even Pa. Even after Grandmum." Thinking about my sister stirs another thought. "Why is everyone okay with girls not getting their own Revealing? How fair is that?"

The dragon's face stretches in what I can only guess is a grin. It's a horrible sight. "Is there a question you wish to ask?"

I take a moment to be sure. "No. I don't think I need to ask anything anymore."

The dragon's claw scrapes away the cooling pool between us. Her form blends back into the darkness.

"Remember this, man-boy," calls the voice as I feel my way back to the crevice. "The truth is best woven one thread at a time."

When I leave the warmth of the cave, I'm surprised to see Elder Borin at the fire instead of Hayden. The sun was sinking when I entered, but now the light is as bright and fresh as morning. How long was I in that cave?

Elder Borin pushes dirt over the cinders then turns to me. "So?"

I take a deep breath. The air tastes moist. It will rain soon. Good. The crops need it. "I think my strength is that I can see truth."

Elder Borin smiles. It doubles the wrinkles on his face, but he looks better that way. "What can you do with truth?"

I remember what the dragon said about the madness of men. "I can accept it. And I can speak it."

Elder Borin nods. "Come. Help an old man back down to the village."

If Elder Borin hiked all this way on his own, he's probably more fit than he lets on, but I extend my arm anyway. As we make our way down the hill I ask, "What trade can I practice in the village with truth as my strength?"

Elder Borin's wrinkles lift into another smile. "How do you feel about being an elder?"

THE GUARDIAN'S MELODY
Zachary Holbrook

Betska stiffened as the enchanting song drifted from the woods. Her half-gutted fish fell from her limp fingers, and she burst out of her dark cottage

Father would be no help. He was deaf to the song, denying its existence even after it took Maer. She needed to find the person most susceptible to its seductive power and keep her safe.

"Laika?" Betska scanned the fields where she'd last seen her little sister playing. Nothing.

Wait—a flash of blue. A tiny figure disappearing beyond the tree line.

Betska dashed after her, cursing herself. She'd grown careless. After years of hearing no music but her own feeble attempts to master Maer's violin, she'd let Laika leave her sight.

The thick underbrush cut at her bare arms as she entered the forest, but she shoved it aside. How long had Maer taken to vanish? She'd been older than Laika was now. She should've known better than to chase songs into the wilderness.

Betska pressed forward. The song tugged at her, notes enshrouding her heart and begging her to follow. A sickly sweet taste rose in her mouth, that of a dark, primal urge the song promised to satisfy. She shuddered and turned away.

No. You have to follow. To find Laika.

Betska relaxed her guard, allowing the melodic tendrils into her soul. The forest parted before her. She walked on damp loam, the music intensifying with every step. Every beat of her hammering heart sent a wave of craving through her veins.

And why should she resist it? Maer had left her for this song.

A few feet away, the underbrush crawled aside, allowing a figure in a sky-blue dress to emerge. Betska froze at the sight of her sister. But Laika walked deeper into the forest with her arms hanging limply by her sides, jaw slack, eyes wide and empty.

The song's hold on Betska shattered, and she grabbed Laika's arm. "We need to leave. *Now*."

Laika shook her head. She scowled and jerked away. "I wanna follow the song!"

"Laika!" Betska reached for her again. "Big sister says come home."

An aggressive series of notes pierced the air, striking Betska with an almost physical force. She flinched and drew back. Laika fled, the music seeming to hurry her along even as it held Betska back. The song rose, drowning out Betska's pleas.

She staggered after her sister, but the song slammed into her, driving her to her knees. The soft, seductive melody that had lured away Maer was gone, replaced by a wrathful pulse.

Pain tore through Betska's abdomen. She cried out and collapsed. The music gnawed within her, tearing her apart. Her organs recoiled against the rhythm, each beat racking her flesh.

But then, a single, discordant note broke through, and then another. They grew into a brilliant, new strain that defied the furious music, sweeping around Betska and washing away her agony. She shuddered and pushed herself up. Was that a *violin*?

The melody grew stronger until it banished the opposing music entirely. Bushes rustled, and the source of the new song emerged—a familiar woman in a dark green dress, violin held against her neck.

Maer.

Betska rose to her feet, reaching out hesitantly. A memory surged before her mind—the corner of the cellar where she'd huddled, hands clamped over her ears, hiding from the song that hunted for her soul. Father returning after hours of searching, his voice hoarse from screaming Maer's name.

Betska touched Maer's cheek. Real. Solid.

She slapped it. "Where have you been? Maer, we needed you!"

Maer recoiled, pain and confusion blossoming across her face. Her violin and bow hung limply at her side.

Betska lowered her hand. "I—I'm sorry."

"No." Maer knelt, resting her violin in a bed of moss that sprung up at her feet. "*I'm* sorry. I knew the sirens' song would only lead to death in the end. I followed it anyway. Only a miracle delivered me."

"Why didn't you come back? Father thought you'd been eaten by a bear!" Betska threw her arms in the air. "We would have welcomed you." She wanted to say more, but the words clumped in her throat.

Have you ever felt an anguish so great it could've torn you in two, except you can't let it, because the pillar of strength you've leaned on ever since Mother died is gone? Because you have to be the big sister now?

"I had new responsibilities," Maer said. "I couldn't return."

"You should've," Betska spat, chest heaving with anger. "What responsibility could be greater than the one you owed to your own kin?"

Have you ever been hunted by fear every time you step outside, a single note enough to fill you with dread?

"There is more than one song in these woods, sister." Maer ran a finger along the edge of her violin. "After the guardian saved me, she asked that I become her apprentice. To learn to play one of those songs."

"That's not a good reason!" Betska bit her lip. *Do you know what you put me through, Maer? What you're putting me through again?*

If you'd stayed, you could have saved Laika.

Betska grabbed her sister's wrist. "This guardian who saved you. Where is she? We need to find—"

"She's dead."

The words snatched away the last of Betska's hope. She crumpled to the ground.

"*I* am the new guardian." Maer took Betska's hand and pulled her to her feet. "That's why I couldn't come home. She was dying when she found me, needed someone to carry on her work. That burden fell on me."

"Fine. Save Laika, then." Betska took a deep breath. "Bring her home to me."

"That's what I came here to do." Maer gave a faint smile. "But I need your help."

"What do you need me to do?"

"What you've always done." Maer retrieved her violin.

"Keep her by your side."

Maer played a slow, contemplative melody. The forest shifted, branches bending backward to create a clear path for Betska to walk through. The music wrapped around her, bathing her in the sounds of the past. For a moment, she could imagine being Laika's age again, listening to Maer while Father sang along in his dusky bass. Her anger at her older sister and her fear for her younger faded into the background.

She *would* save Laika — track these sirens to the ends of the earth and wrest her from their grip, if that's what it took.

Then the other song returned, dark, beckoning. A chill passed through Betska. The bushes before her parted, revealing a cliff stretched out over a misty cove. A waterfall thundered in the distance, vaguely familiar. Ogiv Falls, the terminus of the river where Father fished. Betska swallowed hard. The falls were two day's journey by boat. How had she come so far?

Laika approached the falls from another direction, hands outstretched as if grasping at an invisible stream. The song rose in intensity, no longer beckoning, but demanding. Betska took a trembling step forward. She needed to go, to get to the source of that song. No, to save Laika.

Laika! Laika!

Betska recalled her sticky hands when they'd kneaded dough together, her cheery smile when they'd fetched water from the river. The sirens' song dimmed in her ears.

"Go." Maer rested a hand on Betska's shoulder. "I'm with you."

Betska sprinted toward Laika. Behind her, Maer's melody burst to life, vibrant and powerful. The notes charged into the sirens' song, shattering it.

Laika neared the edge of the cliff. Betska swept her into her arms, skidding to a stop inches from the precipice. Vaguely humanoid figures swirled in the water below, sending the song into the air.

The song regrouped from Maer's attack and struck with renewed ferocity. Betska staggered backward, clutching Laika tight. Laika writhed and kicked. Her eyes were wide, with pinpoint pupils — still in the grip of the sirens.

Laika clawed at Betska's face, drawing blood.

Betska shoved aside the pain and clung to her all the more fiercely. "You're my sister. I will protect you. Laika, please come back to me."

Laika let out a feral cry and lashed out again.

"You are loved," Betska whispered, kneeling in the damp grass and pressing Laika against her chest. The sirens' song thundered behind her, but she felt no compulsion to follow it. "You are loved. You are loved. You are loved."

Maer's battle against the sirens intensified. The strains of the violin rose and fell with increasing speed, each one an arrow aimed at the heart of the dark melody holding Laika captive. Betska drank in the music as it shot over her, and she knew that Maer was pouring out her heart.

Laika kicked, spat, and screamed, but gradually her struggles died down. Maer's song soared in triumph. The sirens fled before it, their own plaintive notes vanishing beneath the waters. Betska breathed deeply, absorbing the last of Maer's music. Relief flooded over her.

She lowered Laika into the grass. The child's eyes opened, and they were her own once more. She stared at Betska for a moment and began to sob.

"Shhh." Betska picked her back up and stood, resting Laika's head against her shoulder. "It's all right. You're safe now."

"I hurt you," Laika choked out. "I'm sorry!"

"I forgive you." Betska stroked Laika's back and strode toward the edge of the woods, where Maer waited her violin held at her side. Maer beamed, then collapsed in the grass.

Betska stifled a cry of alarm and rushed to her side. Maer stared upward, her chest heaving. Sweat streaked her face.

"I'm fine," Maer gasped. "Just tired, that's all."

Betska crouched, setting Laika down. Maer reached to touch Laika's face, and Betska noticed that tiny drops of blood stained the fingers on her left hand.

Maer had poured everything into that song.

"I'll help you home," Betska said, lifting Maer into a sitting position.

Maer shook her head. "I cannot go. When I took up the mantle of the guardian, I… I sacrificed part of my humanity to become something more. I'm invisible to any who cannot hear the songs. Father wouldn't be able to see me."

Laika looked at Betska, face twisted in confusion. "Who is this?"

Maer let out a weak laugh. "I haven't seen you since you were barely walking, Laika. Oh, I missed so much! Stay with me, Betska, until my strength returns, and tell me all that happened in my absence."

Betska glanced toward the sun sinking beneath the cliffs. The events of the past three years tangled within her, a mass of thoughts and feeling too big to force out of her throat. The exhaustion of managing the farm alone on the days that Father sold fish in the market. The joy of watching Laika grow. The hollow void left by Maer. The fear of the song.

"I'll try." Betska picked at the threads of the tangled memories within her and drew them out, one by one. Maer listened intently, joy and sorrow mingling in her eyes.

Betska continued as the sun vanished and Laika curled up and fell asleep in the grass. Her words flowed freely now. There was something intensely *right* about talking to Maer, as if she'd returned to the nights they'd spent awake long past their bedtimes, whispering conspiratorially under covers. She drew words from a deeper part of her soul than she'd intended, words of pain. Loneliness. Anger.

"I'm sorry." Maer pushed herself onto her knees. "I'm so sorry."

"I forgive you." Betska said. The words came automatically, but she meant them. Meant them with every inch of her being.

"You've done so well, Betska!" Maer touched her shoulder. "You've been the sister to Laika that I should've been to you. I saw your love pouring out on her when you held her safe against the sirens' song. You gave her the greatest gift you could."

And you did, too. Maer's bleeding fingers, her willowy frame crumpling after the battle was won...

Betska looked away, biting her lips to stop the tide of emotions from overwhelming her entirely.

Maer pulled her into an embrace and began whispering softly. "You are loved, Betska. You are loved. You are loved. You are loved."

Betska gave in and wept.

☙☙☙

The tree line parted once more, revealing a moonlit cottage on a hill. Betska walked toward home, a sleeping Laika in her aching arms and the fading strains of Maer's music echoing behind her. She glanced back one last time to see Maer wave and fade into the woods. Betska nodded after her.

The back door creaked open at her touch, and Betska stepped inside. A dark figure slumped at the table.

"Father?" Betska whispered.

The figure lifted his head, revealing haggard features and red-rimmed eyes. He stared in shock for a moment, then let out a weary laugh—a song to Betska's heart.

Father stumbled forward and practically crushed them in his arms. Laika stirred, rubbing her eyes with an annoyed cry.

Betska smiled and lowered her to the floor. She'd explain to Father what happened. Perhaps he'd believe this time. Perhaps not. Either way, she'd continue listening closely for any hint of a song—not out of fear of the sirens, but in hope of hearing the joyous, hopeful strains of the guardian's melody.

THE HEART OF A SHADOW
Tracey Dyck

I straddle a low bough of the Glade's single tree, my chapped fingers clumsy from cold as I knot a string around a branch. Wind frees dark tendrils of hair from my hood.

The other end of the string is already tied securely around a heart. No beat, no warmth. Just a crystalline, fist-shaped organ radiating a blue glow. I stare into its fading light, searching for the memories within.

But I sense nothing. Just the oily slick of shadow clinging to my palms.

Working with shadows is difficult. They're harmless until they claim a human heart and take on a solid shape that can rip and tear, maim and kill. As a warden, I've seen tigers, stags, and men with wings in these mountains. Today it was a bear, made from the same slippery darkness as all the rest.

We may never oust the shadows from Duphana, but we can guard the hearts of our slain. We can reclaim what the shadows steal from us.

I scoot forward on the branch and let this heart dangle among hundreds of others. One blue light amidst greens, violets, ambers, and reds. They stir in the wind and chime a forlorn melody, their colors rippling over the frozen waterfalls enclosing the Glade on all sides. Here, the tree's ancient magic protects them, but any visiting wardens would be vulnerable to attack.

"Kila?" The guard standing at the only entrance to the Glade, a passageway between two sheer ice walls, glances up at the dark clouds riding a fast-moving cold front. "Better get home soon, yeah?"

"In a moment," I call back. My fists are clenched, fingertips numb. I should be able to sense every heart hanging from these branches. There once was a time I would sit in this tree and weep, laugh, *feel* the fragments of these lives gone before me. The missing echoes should make me weep now, but I cannot.

My chest is hollow.

Somewhere out there, my own heart sits in a box made of stone. Alive but apart from me. Small price to pay. If I'd kept it, it would've shattered into a million pieces long ago from the grief. For the sake of my friend, I can't afford that.

"One day your heart will return to its rightful place, too, Sathii." I repeat this vow every time I bring someone else's heart to the Glade's tree to honor their memory. It's been a year since her death. The shadow that stole her heart is probably long gone. But I haven't stopped looking.

The guard turns to face me again. "Kila, come on."

"Coming." I start to climb down, ready to go home and sleep off the growing heaviness tugging at my limbs, but a snarl rips across the Glade.

A pitch-black shadow creature charges through the passageway on two hooved feet. Curled ram's horns, long teeth jutting from its lower lip. It falls upon the guard before he can even raise his crossbow.

I leap down, my twin daggers drawn before my boots hit the snow.

The creature's teeth rake through the guard's neck, and he drops.

I hurl a dagger too late. The tip bounces off one of the beast's horns, and the monster turns toward me. Within its dark figure, white light flickers. I stumble, second knife poised over my shoulder.

White like Sathii's hair that I used to braid. Is that her heart?

I snap off the memory like an icicle before it can burrow into my veins, and I hurl my second knife. It thunks into the creature's broad shoulder.

With a keening howl, the shadow flees back down the passageway.

I bolt to the guard's side. His throat is weeping red into the snow. My whole body shakes as I pull off my scarf to stop the bleeding, but the wound is too wide, and his blank eyes stare unseeing at the sky. Do I even remember his name? How can I grieve his death if I can't feel a thing? All I can think is that I distracted him. If I hadn't been here, he'd have seen the monster coming.

Move, Kila. Or a shadow will come to take his heart, and you'll have another monster on your hands.

I pick up my fallen dagger, then lift the guard's body over my shoulders. My back strains against his weight, and warmth seeps down my arm as I stagger out of the Glade. The instant I leave the shelter of the ice walls behind, wind slaps me like the palm of a giant hand, and I nearly drop the guard.

Hoof prints lead to the left, up into the heights, where the coming storm ushers in an early evening. In the distance, the shadow's loping form disappears into the trees. I bite back a curse. If there's even the slightest chance that thing is carrying Sathii's heart, I have to get it back.

But first I have to bring this guard's body to safety. He doesn't deserve to have his heart stolen, too.

With one last look to pin down the creature's direction, I head to the right, where the village of Duphana sits curled at the mountain's base like a stone dragon puffing smoke from scores of chimneys. The scent of venison stew carries on the air, but mixed with the copper tang of the guard's blood, it does nothing but make my empty stomach twist.

I'm only half aware of the downward trek leading to my village's streets.

Heavy footsteps cut through the fog. "Kila! What's going on? What happened to Jado?"

I look up. It's another guard with a red scarf hiding all but his eyes.

"A shadow," I pant. My throat is raw. "Must've made it past the perimeter watch. The Glade's unguarded now. Send in a replacement and take this man to secure his heart." I let the body slide to the street. "I have to go."

"Wait!" He grabs my arm. "Looks like a mean one blowing in. Are you sure…" He looks to the mountains, edging away from the event we all remember too well.

Sathii and I, fresh-faced wardens on a shadow hunt, were caught in the mountains during last winter's fiercest storm. An avalanche was on top of us before we knew it. I made it. She didn't.

They dug out her body four days later when the blizzard passed, but shadows don't need to dig. One seeped through the snow and took her heart, leaving hoof prints in the drifts as the only sign it had been there. Hoof prints exactly like the ones I saw today.

I fasten the guard with a heavy stare and hope it doesn't reveal the cracks in my walls. "Let me go," I say quietly.

My rank is enough to make his hand fall, and I leave him to pick up the corpse.

No time to restock supplies. I wipe my bloody hands on my coat, tug on my fur-lined gloves, and sprint back the way I came. Several hundred yards outside of Duphana, I find the hoof prints again and shoulder into the northern gale, head down.

As darkness falls, the snow deepens against the mountainside, turning my sprint into an uphill trudge. Wind howls in my ears and pierces my coat.

Lungs heaving, I rest for a moment in the shelter of an enormous pine tree. I should go back before this storm gets any worse. But I promised Sathii, her family, myself. I promised I'd get her heart back. The thought of it fueling that bloodthirsty monster pushes me out of my shelter.

An hour later, white light flickers ahead. I dash forward—but it's gone.

Tracing a wide circle reveals no prints or snapped branches. As the falling snow thickens around me and my toes turn to ice in my boots, I am stripped of all that makes me a warden. Eyesight obscured. Strength waning. Tracking skills nullified as the snow fills in any prints the monster might've left.

My teeth clench so hard that my jaws ache. I haven't been this cold since the day I followed the rumors of the Crypt Keeper to the top of this mountain and asked him to extract my living heart from my chest.

I wonder how much strength he's sapped from it in the past year.

But this is my insurance against the shadows. Without my heart, I am invincible. If I should die out here, the shadows will find nothing to take. I'm an empty body, a shadow-slaying machine. For Sathii's sake, I am heartless.

Sathii wouldn't want me empty.

I choke on freezing air and tumble to my knees. The blizzard is blinding, merciless. A few trees rise as dark sentinels.

I sink into the snow, spent, dimly aware of whiteness already drifting over my legs to bury me. Maybe I should let it. I could join Sathii in death.

A real warden could find her heart.

That's because a real warden could track her memories. But I can't anymore. The mere thought of reliving my past locks my joints and sucks the air from my lungs. If I were to plunge that fragile organ back into my chest, I'd break from the memories before I ever found her. If only I was strong enough to reclaim my heart.

Strong enough not to drown in all I've lost.

"I miss you." The words are swallowed by the storm.

It's true—I remember her, but only with my head. The part of me that knew her embrace and her laugh and her ridiculous jokes is gone. It's locked in a box at the top of this peak.

Without it, I'll never find her. I need to get it back.

I push up on trembling legs. Tighten my hood. Turn in what feels like an upward direction. One slogging step after another, pressing higher, though I can't see the way.

My training comes back to haunt me, warning that one misstep could send me plunging down an unseen cliff, where my body will break on the rocks and the shadows will try and fail to scavenge me.

I can't feel my hands or feet. Darkness lies so deep over the mountainside that I can barely see the swirling whiteout. My legs fail me, and I collapse again.

But the blizzard abates for a moment. And there, shining in the moonlight as clouds shred apart, is the crypt—a squat, stone building teetering on an overhang at least thirty yards up.

On hands and knees, I scale the slope and drag myself through the open door.

A fire blazes inside the room, lending an angry, orange light to the dozens of stone boxes in the walls' alcoves. I crawl closer, but I can't feel the fire's warmth. I can't feel anything.

A voice slithers out from the corner. "Whhhhyyyy are you hhhere?" The Crypt Keeper steps into the light, swathed in pale robes. The crystals pierced through his brow, nose, and ears look like shattered pieces of long-dead hearts. "You have nothing more to offer me."

"I... want it back." I gasp on the floor. Was it only a year ago when I stood here shuddering as he plunged his hand into my chest as easily as I reach into shadows? When he tore a violet crystal from between my ribs and left me both vacant and brave?

"Our agreement was ssssealed. Why risk losing your place in the Glade?" The years he's stolen from countless hearts like mine have carved ravines into his face.

"I'll pay any price." I reach a shaking hand for the fire, suddenly aching with the loss of touch. Even now, there is no prickle of pain from the heat—there's nothing, and for the first time in a year, I see this howling void inside me for what it is. "I just... want my heart."

"I will return it to the people of Duphana upon your death, and they can hang it in the Glade where it belongs. As we agreed. Until then, it's mine."

"I want it back *now*. While I still live."

"No."

Something snaps in that hollow place within me. I thrust my hand into the fire and raise a flaming log. Flesh sizzles, but I can't feel the burn bubbling into my palm. I hurl the log, and it strikes the Keeper's head.

He stumbles back with a bellow, then lunges at me.

His weight knocks me to the floor. His hand closes around my throat. Mine closes around my second dagger.

I've carved open too many chests to miss. The blade slips between his ribs, and I watch the life leave his eyes. He crumples to the side like a flag cut loose.

I rise, unsteady, and take an iron key from around his neck. My alcove is the twenty-first one on the fourth row from the bottom. The stone box inside is locked, but the key fits perfectly.

Inside lies a glassy organ pulsing with violet light. I fumble for it with senseless fingers. With the Keeper gone, there's no going back.

Holding my breath, I press the heart against my chest. And as it disappears inside, searing heat sinks through my skin—then floods my being, roaring into every nerve.

I am tearing apart. Images assault my mind, memories wrapped in sounds, tastes, and inexplicable grief.

Sathii beating me to the top of the ice walls, only to climb back down to lend me one of her tools when mine jams.

Giving me flatbread, lumpy and tasteless but warm in my empty stomach.

Laughing across the mountain chasms.

Tears freezing on her cheeks as she holds me in my darkest moments.

Her last words practical and kind as she wraps her scarf around my neck just before the avalanche hurtles down the mountain.

Her body excavated from the snow, face blue and fingers black. Heart gone.

The years pound into me. I am wracked with sobs until it seems my ribcage will fracture. My hand screams from the burn now, and the world is dark because Sathii is no longer in it.

This is the darkness I feared. I am drowning, gasping for air as my tears drip to the stone floor, and my ruined hand curls to my chest to feel my thundering pulse at last.

That's when all the memories spool into a thread, tightening around me and pulling me forward.

I find myself standing outside in the wind-whipped snow, flakes pelting my cheeks to mingle with my tears. My sobs shrink until they're nothing but a halting hitch in my throat.

Sathii's echoes stretch before me in an invisible cord — a cord that I feel with every fiber of my grief-torn being. It cuts straight through me and leads down into the darkness.

Far below, a shadow stirs, and in its midst flickers a white light.

DRIFT
Roystonn Pruitt

Code's sprint through the access corridor broke into a stumble as the ship lurched hard from a muffled explosion. He pursed his lips and continued, albeit with plugged ears as the loud screech of metal grinding against metal filled the air—no doubt the secondary generators dying. As if that wasn't loud enough, alarms and shouting added to the cacophony.

The corridor flickered and went dark, but red emergency light quickly kicked in. The ship jolted from another muffled explosion, and multiple smaller pops rattled the walls and floors.

A reverberating, digitized voice came in through the intercoms, drowning out the shouting. "Reactors offline. Emergency power activated. Total power loss in aft section. Pressure in aft section at fifty percent and dropping. Attitude control offline. Extensive repairs needed to maintain orbital trajectory."

"You kidding me?" Code droned as he dodged several other crew. He approached a junction to a perpendicular corridor and prepared to hook a left.

"Attitude control?" scoffed a deep and rough female voice from around the corner. "My wrench will cure any attitude problems."

Code's boots skidded against the floor, slowing him just in time and sparing a collision. A good catch, considering her muscular, seven-foot-tall frame and menacing, canine complexion. Gendrilo were not to be trifled with, at least physically. Verbally, however, Code was feeling adventurous. "It means the ship's orientation, not literal attitude!"

Visibly flustered, Lergra snapped back, "It was a joke! Must I also adjust *your* attitude?"

She stormed into a nearby maintenance room, her tailwinds twisting the now-plentiful smoke into vortices. At this, Code took his left turn and sprinted to a wall console farther down the corridor.

Once there, he pressed a few buttons to prepare a socket for the auxiliary power conduit that Lergra would be delivering soon.

But to his horror, the access hatch wouldn't budge.

Seconds later, Lergra emerged from the room, dragging the heavy cable behind her. "Code! Tell me the socket is ready!"

"It would be," Code shouted back, "if the hatch wasn't stuck!"

Lergra continued down the corridor, bringing the cable closer with each labored footstep. Her expression carried no shortage of sarcastic sweetness, and the colorful, shaggy fur on her neck collected onto one shoulder as she tilted her dog-like head. "Ohh, have your puny Human arms failed you again? Must Lergra lift for you once more?"

Code returned her expression with one of exaggerated cheerfulness that didn't quite mask the contempt beneath it. "By all means, I happily invite you to use your infinite Gendrilo strength to assist."

"No need," interrupted another male voice approaching from the other end of the corridor. It was digitized similarly to the one from the intercom, but deeper and possessing a particularly arrogant flavor. "My expertise will fix it, unlike your uneducated bickering."

A spindly, metal android shooed Code away from the console and took his place. He pressed a few buttons and turned a knob, and the hatch ascended.

With a gentle whirring of gears, the android turned his head and focused his eye-like sensors onto Code, then Lergra. "If you fleshlings would consider all the options at your disposal, much more would be accompli—*Ack!*"

Lergra shoved the android aside with her shaggy, barb-tipped tail. "Silly Foli. Always talking. Always in the way."

She shunted the cable into the socket and twisted a coupling into place, then pressed a few other buttons on the console. The red emergency glow gave way to the brilliance of the standard bulkhead lights.

Lergra planted her fists onto her wide hips and flashed a

toothy smile. "Mental strength. Muscle strength. It's still strength. My point has been proven, appliance."

Foli raised a finger in protest, but Code spoke first. "And you know what else needs proving? Our ability to get the attitude control online. That is, unless you enjoy the delicious smell of barbecue as we enter the atmosphere."

As if prompted by his words, the intercom called out, "Warning, decaying orbit. Adjust trajectory."

Lergra narrowed the long tufts of fur that served as her eyebrows, their tan color contrasting the black, brown, and white patches covering the rest of her body. "Point taken."

Foli pushed past Lergra and went for the keyboard next to the cable socket. His metal fingers skittered across the keys, opening a top-down diagram of the ship. The entire aft section, and every attitude control bay and escape pod, was flashing red. He brought up the attitude control menu, and a diagnostic indicated complete disconnection and severe damage. Full replacements were needed.

Foli sighed. "An inconvenient amount of damage. Some might say devastating."

Code pursed his lips. "Lots of red. No movement, no escape. *Totally* not sabotage. Nope."

"Surprised I haven't seen or heard the captain since this mess started." Lergra pressed the vocal interface button on the console. "Dial Captain Laqacen."

An artificial voice responded over the speaker, "Captain Laqacen phone disconnected."

"Okay, where is Captain Laqacen?"

"Captain Laqacen not detected. Last known position: engine bay."

"Not detected? Dial engine bay."

"Engine bay disconnected."

Lergra glared at the console. "Full status report of engine bay."

"Full disconnect. Zero power. Zero pressure. Zero gravity. Access not recommended without extravehicular protection."

Lergra disconnected the call. "Captain's dead, and the engine bay is probably an expanding cloud of debris."

Code threw his hands in the air. "What a wuss, choosing

death instead of being productive."

"Productivity in mind," added Foli, striding away from the other two with increasing speed, "command might be our best bet. If we cannot prevent loss of orbit, perhaps we can control it while in atmosphere."

Code followed. "I see what you're getting at. Ride it down, use the ailerons and brake fins."

"And avoid becoming a new surface feature visible from space," added Lergra. "Also wouldn't want to land on any civilizations. That would be rude."

"Implying aliens actually exist." Code twisted his expression with sarcastic incredulity.

Lergra produced a bellowing, sarcastic laugh. "Ahh, of course, of course! Everyone knows they don't! I was being silly."

"Perhaps it would be better to crash," Foli remarked dryly, clearly unamused by their banter.

Code and the others scrambled down the corridor toward the bow, dodging the other crew who now had a bit more panic in their steps. They passed through the final doorway, and the spherical command room sprawled out before them. Viewscreens covered the inner surface seamlessly, granting an omni-directional projection of the surrounding space and digitally transforming the rest of the ship into ghostly outlines.

External floodlights illuminated the stern where large chunks of hot debris and smoky haze drifted away in every direction, including engine fragments. From the bow, the black surface of a sunless world loomed entirely too close for comfort.

The command room floor was sparsely populated by the few crew who could man the control kiosks, and the navigation seat was vacant. Capitalizing on this, Foli planted his artificial rear on the seat and brought up the relevant console, then tapped some buttons. "Seems we still have access to the entry systems. Code and Lergra, strap in and try not to let the sum of your parts drop below its current value."

Code took his place in the seat next to Foli and did as instructed, tugging at the straps and making sure each one was secure. He felt the floor heave a little as Lergra took the seat behind his. "Commencing *Meteor Simulator: Deluxe Edition*."

"Does the game have a cheat code for invincibility?" Lergra

asked. "I need to make sure you get me the barbecue you promised."

Code kept his eyes ahead, although one of them twitched. "I promised nothing. I mentioned barbecue as a metaphor."

"Ah, so 'metaphor' also means 'broken promise?'"

"Please cease the noise-making," Foli requested before activating the ship's comms. "This is acting captain Folinl dabaGesh advising the remaining crew to please secure yourselves, as the ship is about to undergo atmospheric entry. Fleshlings should be especially wary of loose objects, including themselves. Nobody wants viscera littering the floor."

"This so-called 'fleshling' will be keeping her viscera, thank you," Lergra said sharply.

Code glared. "Those words belong in a horror movie."

Foli pressed a few buttons, prompting advisory alarms to sound throughout the ship. "They garner appropriate attention, do they not?"

Code felt the ship accelerate gradually as the planet drew closer, and a persistent vibration began rattling his bones. Outside, glowing streaks and wisps of superheated air streamed past, and nearby chunks of debris ignited into a lightshow of meteors.

He gripped his chair tighter as Foli teased the controls with precision, adjusting the still-functional ailerons to ensure that the ship stayed on a reasonably straight path. Another keystroke deployed the airbrakes, and the digital outlines of dozens of metal flaps rose from the ship's skin like scales on a lizard.

More debris streaked past as the ship slowed. Much-needed relief washed over Code for a brief moment before a loud crash and a hard jolt shattered it. Several more crashes followed, and alarms filled the air while the ship started spinning.

"Oh, silly me," said Foli, his voice carrying nary a hint of concern, though this was not reflected by his frantic keystrokes on the console.

Code's already-frayed nerves unraveled further with the, "Silly *you*?" blurted by Lergra next to his left ear.

"There was some debris trailing behind us," Foli continued. "Normally the sensors in the rear of the ship would have notified me of impending collision, but since the rear no longer exists, the event reached its logical conclusion."

"Speaking of conclusions," added Code as his mind spun with the rest of the ship, "ours seems to be too close for comfort. How is the—"

"A minor glitch," Foli interrupted. "Fixing."

Code watched a top-down diagram of the ship appear on Foli's monitor, and all the airbrakes retracted. They redeployed on one side, returning stability, then redeployed on the other side.

On the forward screens, a neon grid representation of the rapidly approaching landscape appeared. The debris ahead of the ship was already peppering the landscape, creating tiny flashes of chaos.

"On to act two of the performance," said Foli, pressing a few more buttons. "The airbrakes were successful. Deploying hardlight chutes now."

Keeping his eyes on the monitor, Code saw a series of shimmering asterisms appear around the diagram, making it resemble a giant pinecone. More chunks of debris streaked past as the ship lurched and leveled out, putting it almost parallel to the ground.

Lergra's voice filled Code's left ear again, "If we survive this, I'll expect my barbecue."

Code rolled his eyes and nodded sharply in concession. "Fine, we'll have barbecue!"

Seeing the landscape draw closer until he could pick out the details of hills and cliffs, Code grimaced and braced for impact.

"If you weren't holding on before, now is the time," Foli announced as he pressed an exceptionally large, red button.

Just before closing his eyes, Code saw hardlight sleds appear beneath the now side-oriented diagram of the ship.

He could have sworn his skeleton had been flung from his body in the initial impact, and several more jolts told him that they were skipping like a rock. A grinding vibration persisted for what felt like minutes, gradually lessening until sound and movement ceased.

Code opened his eyes and released his iron grip from his seat's armrests. He saw a dark landscape from the still-functioning screens, but no mangled wreck. He cracked a smile.

"Ha! What a ride. Nice flying, slick."

He turned to face Foli, but the android and his seat were missing.

Lergra laughed and pointed to the front of the bridge. "The appliance ragdolled over there."

Code unbuckled himself and ran with Lergra to inspect. Foli's eye lights were off, indicating deactivation.

Code shook him by the shoulders. "Hey, Foli. Wake up. It's time for breakfast."

"You know quite well that I don't eat breakfast, or any other repulsive, corporeal food."

The voice, wispy like a leaky steam valve, had not come from Foli's body, but next to Code's left ear. He turned his head and saw not a robot, but a ghostly fog with three faintly glowing slivers for eyes arranged in a radial pattern — the gaseous *body* of a fothWurrq.

Code stood. "*There* you are. Did your suit break?"

"The impact activated the ejection mechanism. I thought I had fixed that."

"Don't float around naked," said Lergra, scowling. "You tempt me to get the desk fan. Get dressed, and let's go out to survey the damage."

Foli huffed before funneling himself through a small access port in the suit's chest. The eye lights flickered back on as his limbs twitched to life. He stood, and Code led them to the expeditionary equipment room. They donned their environment suits, gathered the relevant gear, and made their way to the nearest airlock.

The door slid shut behind them, sealing them in. The room vented the air with a hiss and replaced it with the thin, xenon-based atmosphere from outside.

Code twisted and pulled a handle, opening the outer door. A gangway extended down to the mysterious, icy landscape, and he led his team to the surface.

Floodlights illuminated the hot debris that littered the path carved by the landing skids. Atop the ship, a communication mast had been extended as a distress beacon, and Code felt his spirits rise accordingly.

The ship's extensive damage was a sight to behold, but

Code's attention turned to the ground. He saw not dirt or stone, but a patchwork of artificial tiles, and the ones that weren't coated in dust or ice had an opalescent luster that revealed ornate carvings.

Foli cleared the ice off a tile with one of his feet. "Fascinating."

"The remains of an alien civilization." Code spread his arms as if presenting something grand. "Imagine that! Aliens!"

Lergra laughed. "I know, yes? Who knew there was other life in the universe? Nobody will believe us!"

Code and Lergra laughed with an arm over the other's shoulder. A glimpse at Foli's motionless, judgmental stare told Code that the android wasn't likely to adopt their *fleshling* humor anytime soon, and that cultural contrast would never cease to be entertaining.

Saying nothing, Foli rotated his head 360 degrees, likely inspecting the surrounding area for more evidence of these proposed aliens. The swiveling stopped in the direction of a nearby cliffside.

"Perhaps you can laugh while walking," said Foli, pointing to his new target. "Those ruins over there are sure to provide more amusement."

Code and Lergra turned to the cliff and beheld outlines of buildings carved out of the side.

"More interesting than our mining contract," said Lergra.

"And probably more lucrative," Code added. "Let's do this."

Lergra loomed over him, "But not as a distraction from the barbecue, Hacody Beckern."

"Wouldn't dream of it," he said while dismissively waving a hand and walking forward. Despite her intimidating body language, he knew a smile sat upon her shadowed face. "After this, we'll have a cookout."

THE UGLY CRONE
Karen Avizur

"They pinned me to the chair," the man whispered, his glassy eyes staring at his hands in his lap. "Took blood samples. It felt like days, but it could've been hours. It was so bright. I could barely see anything. And I kept... I kept screaming, but they didn't stop..."

Katherine Holloway looked up from her laptop. "I think I've got everything I need."

He slid his eyes up to hers. "You don't believe me."

Katherine sighed wearily. "No, Mr. McGregor, and do you know why?"

"I don't *know* why there aren't marks where they—"

"That's not it."

"You think I'm *lying*?" Mr. McGregor snapped.

"No, you completely believe what you're saying," Katherine told him. "That's not the problem. The problem is the spaceship that you say idled outside your window without anyone else in the apartment building, or San Diego, or anyone in the US military for that matter, noticing it."

The sixty-odd-year-old man shoved himself to his feet, sending the chair screeching backwards across the floor. "Fine. I knew the feds wouldn't believe me, anyway." At that, he turned and stalked out of the room.

Katherine shook her head as she closed his interview form on her laptop and then opened up a fresh one. Light footfalls entered the room, and when Katherine looked up, her eyes met an unassuming teenage girl shutting the door behind her.

"Hi," Katherine said.

"Hey." The girl offered a quick wave before folding her hands at her waist. Her thick brown hair was held back in a frizzy ponytail. She sat down in the rolling chair on the other side of the table, putting down the form she'd filled out while waiting in the next room.

Katherine hesitated before picking up the paper. "Rachel Casseus..." She gave it a thorough once-over. "Isn't it a school day?"

"Yeah."

Katherine's eyes flicked back up to the girl. "Why don't you explain to me why you're here?"

Rachel shifted in her seat. "I wrote it all down for you."

"Yes, but I prefer to hear it from you," she answered. "Usually gets me more details."

Rachel swallowed, looking down to her hands. "My brother's been sick a while," she whispered. "In his head. Something... Well, he's in a mental ward. And I went to visit him yesterday with my mom. And... there's something wrong. I mean, more wrong than usual. They've been hurting him in there. One person has. One of the doctors."

"Do you have a name?" Katherine asked.

Rachel shook her head, looking up. "Harvey doesn't remember who it is, or he'd tell me. He can't. That's what I mean; something's messed with his head, so he can't remember."

"Why come to the FBI? Why not tell your mom?"

"I *did* tell her." Annoyance sharpened her tone. "She thinks I'm imagining things."

"Imagining things?" Katherine asked. "So, Harvey didn't actually tell you what's happening to him?"

"I just know something's wrong." Rachel started to tear up. "They're hurting him. He's getting worse. He was never like this at home. He's babbling about things that sound straight out of a nightmare, like there's whole other worlds in his head."

"You didn't answer my question."

Rachel blinked. "Which one?"

"Why come to the FBI?"

"Because someone is *making* him forget what they're doing to him! I know they are!" The teenager averted her gaze. "You don't believe me."

"I believe you," Katherine said. "But this is going to be like pulling teeth if you don't just come out and tell me the truth."

"I am!"

"I mean the *whole* truth. The part where you knew your brother's being hurt because you're clairvoyant."

Rachel froze. The blood slowly drained from her face. "How'd you know that?"

"Why don't you read my mind and find out?" Katherine asked, motioning with her hand.

Hesitating for a moment, Rachel reached out toward the agent and startled. "How are you doing that?"

"How do you think?" Katherine smiled. "You and Harvey aren't the only psychics in this world, Rachel. Far from it. You had to know some work for the FBI."

Rachel remained silent for a long moment before speaking. "I know my brother, Agent Holloway. Something is wrong."

ఞఞఞ

She makes me feel things. The most gut-wrenchingly horrific things. And she pulls out my life, draining me, sucking energy from my mind and body as pins and needles slice deep inside where her hand makes contact with my forehead.

She invents tragedies. She creates worlds in my mind and then destroys them when she's done. Eventually, the things she's changed fade, like a dream I forget when I wake up. But the wrongness of it, the scars, the horrifying roller coaster — they stay with me, and eventually, the chaos bleeds into my reality. My emotions are twisted and contorted, forced into illogical paths in my brain. She manipulates me like I'm a toy to be played with.

My mouth is wide open as I scream, but she doesn't let any sound come out.

ఞఞఞ

Katherine sat shotgun as Special Agent John Sweeney drove up the hospital's long, paved driveway and found a parking spot without too much trouble.

He glanced to her as they made their way inside. "You getting anything?" he signed with his hands.

"No, but that doesn't mean there's nothing here," Katherine signed back, speaking aloud as she did so.

"How can I help you?" asked the woman at the front desk.

"FBI, Special Agents Holloway and Sweeney," Katherine told her as they showed their credentials. She glanced down at the nameplate on her desk. "Sarah Garrison, is it? We're here on report of suspicious behavior. Would it be possible to speak to Dr. Porter?" The woman's eyes widened at their badges, and she hesitated before picking up the phone and sending a page over the PA system. "Can you please also call down all the staff?" Katherine asked.

"Ah... I suppose," she muttered. After Sarah sent out the second page, she looked from Sweeney to Katherine and back. "What's this about?" she asked, getting to her feet.

"We've received a complaint from a guardian about one of your patients," Sweeney spoke aloud.

"What kind of... complaint?" Sarah asked. "Is one of the doctors hurting the patients?"

"That's what we're here to find out," Sweeney replied as several staff entered the room.

Katherine shifted to get Sweeney's attention, and his focus snapped to where she was looking. A young female nurse's eyes locked on Katherine's, something recognized, and suddenly Katherine was drawing her weapon. The young woman grabbed one of the other doctors and shoved him between them before taking off running.

"Move!" Katherine yelled as she darted forward after her target. Sweeney was immediately on her tail, his gun at the ready.

Katherine took a hard left as the young woman darted down a hallway and into a stairwell. She slapped Sweeney on the arm to get his attention and signed *psychic vampire*. At that, his free hand went to his hearing aids, turning them off.

The suspect ducked through a doorway and slammed it shut. The two agents got there seconds later — an eternity — by which time the woman had already engaged a lock.

Katherine cursed, then shut her eyes, reaching out quickly to the minds of those around her — those who were intensely familiar with the layout of the hospital. After a long second, her eyes flew open, and she bolted to her right, Sweeney still right behind her.

They took the stairs quickly, bursting out onto the second floor.

"Shoot your partner!"

The call came out loud and clear from maybe ten yards away, just barely around the corner.

The persuasion washed over Katherine harmlessly and went through Sweeney like his ears weren't even there. Katherine smiled as she and Sweeney came to an abrupt stop at the corner of the hall. All the vampire had done was give away her location. *Shoot your partner*, Katherine signed to Sweeney with an expression that was part grin, part smirk. Sweeney grinned back at her.

A moment later, Katherine took the corner wide, her weapon up and at the ready. She swept each of the rooms she passed, now in the dorm. Just as she realized that, Katherine felt the mind of a panicked patient. Quickening her pace, she flew from left to right, her gun following her gaze, and then she froze. Sweeney stepped to her side, but she waved him off to sweep the area of any interruptions.

A young boy, possibly twelve years old, stood clutching the arm around his throat that was barely allowing him to stand on tiptoe. His eyes were red from a stream of tears, desperation and fear palpable in his expression. Katherine's gun remained trained on the forehead of the perpetrator, who was holding a knife to the boy's neck with her other hand. "Back off," she shouted. "Put your gun on the—"

Katherine pulled the trigger, sending a bullet through the woman's head, and she and Harvey collapsed to the ground.

"It's okay," Katherine said as the boy scrambled away from his attacker, his back hitting the wall. He let out a gut-wrenching scream, putting his fists to his mouth, furiously blinking back tears. "Harvey, look at me, sweetheart. You're safe. Rachel sent us."

Harvey's blinking turned into a flutter, then he hid his face in his hands as he let out a whimper. Katherine mentally reached out toward Harvey, brushing up against some vague identifying information. He had some locked doors for sure, but more than that, his mind was baffling. It was intense. It was frightening.

"What did she do to you?" Katherine whispered.

Harvey trailed his hands down his face as he pulled his knees up to his chest. "It's a maze. It's a puzzle," he mumbled, fidgeting with a loose thread at the bottom of his sweatpants. "It's a game. And she always wins."

Katherine's heart sank as she stared at the young boy, his eyes flitting around every which way like there were things only he could see fluttering about. She turned to the door, where

Sweeney stood, staring wide-eyed at the petrified young boy. "Just a minute," she told him. He nodded once.

Harvey looked to the psychic vampire, dead on the floor. "You slayed the dragon. She tried to hurt me." Harvey looked to Katherine's gun holstered at her side. "Can I see your sword?"

"Not... right now. Can you come with me?" Katherine asked quietly, holding out her hand. "I'm here to take you home."

"I *am* home," Harvey told her, his gaze falling to the floor, his expression sliding into emptiness. "Home is here. I live here. In my room. I'll always live here." For some reason, his eyes shot to Sweeney, and he screamed, fumbling backwards farther. "Will he kill me?" Harvey sobbed. "I don't want to die again–"

"You're safe! He's my friend. He was here to slay the dragon, too."

Katherine took small steps forward along the ground toward the young boy. She realized, though, that Harvey didn't seem to mind any physical movements she made. It was as if only the things in his head mattered. And since Katherine had completely locked herself down so she wouldn't be a burden on the young psychic, she wasn't a threat.

"Harvey, nobody is going to hurt you."

"People *always* hurt you."

Katherine clenched her teeth, trying to figure out the best way to manage the situation—to rectify the dichotomy between how Harvey experienced his surroundings and what was reality. A sudden hatred welled up inside her. The vampire was dead, she'd *killed* her. And yet, a part of her still lived within the boy's mind—burrowed deep, instilling fear that would cling to him for a long time. Rooting it out completely might take years. But for now, Katherine just needed to get through to him. That was the first and most crucial step.

"Harvey, can you look at me, please?" she asked. The young boy lifted his gaze obediently. Katherine nodded slowly. "What do you see in this room, sweetheart? Where are we?"

Harvey's eyes gradually left Katherine's face as he looked around the room. "It's a castle. We're at the top. We're locked in here; not allowed out. And the dragon that was guarding it is dead. But there's always more dragons..."

"I can take you out, if you want," Katherine murmured. "I'll protect you. My partner Sweeney will protect you, too. If anything else tries to hurt you… we will keep you safe. Can you trust me?" Harvey's mouth twitched slightly as he gave Katherine another good once-over, his focus landing on her gun and staying there. "Harvey… take my hand."

    The young boy stared at Katherine for a long while, and then he reached out for her.

THE PLAGUE DRAGON
J.L. Ender

"Lost? We're not lost. I know exactly where we are." I took a deep breath of fresh, country air. Fragrant acacia trees lined the road, each one studded with hundreds of small, spherical yellow flowers. The buds swayed in a gentle breeze.

I patted my horse's neck. "There's a good girl."

My squire Tobias turned to me, shading his eyes from the afternoon sun. "Okay, where are we, then?"

Oh, ye of little faith!

"Well?" he pressed.

I cleared my throat. "Rome."

"Oh, the whole of the Roman Empire! That narrows it down. Great!" He threw up his hands in disgust.

"There's a city ahead. They probably know which corner of Rome we've discovered."

"I wouldn't count on it."

"That's why *I'm* in charge. I know how to look on the bright side."

"Yes. The bright side that got us captured by the Moors in Spain. And got us lost in the catacombs under Paris. And—"

"That'll do. We're wandering knights. If you don't like questing, you're welcome to go back to your desk in London, counting other peoples' money."

Tobias shivered, but said nothing.

We rode in silence over the next two hills.

The stench wrinkled my nose before I saw the source. A broad, dirty pond stretched away to our right as we neared the city, its stagnant water stained with algae, dirt, and an unwholesome, miasmic purple slime. Something shifted under the surface. *A large fish, probably.*

"Oh, yes, this town's going to have *all* the answers." I could practically *feel* Tobias rolling his eyes. "This is going to be worse than Madrid. At least we got away from the Moors not smelling like an abandoned latrine."

"It's... I'm sure the town itself is lovely." I grimaced, hoping I was right.

The city was humble by our standards, with several large clusters of conjoined mud-brick houses divided by a broad, central street. A large palace rose on the far side of town atop a grassy hill.

Villagers gathered at a square near the center of town. I grinned at Tobias, waggling my eyebrows. He scowled at me and shrugged. I took that as assent to approach and led the way.

The townspeople clustered around a dais, silent. A man in fine robes stood on the raised platform behind a massive urn striped red and yellow. A small circlet of a crown sat upon his salt-and-pepper hair.

On the far side of the dais, almost removed from the proceedings, a slim woman with black hair watched, lips pressed into a solemn line. She wore a black dress and, like the apparent king, a simple circlet for a crown.

"I will now draw a name," the king said gravely. He scanned the crowd as he spoke, thick brows furrowed.

An attendant blindfolded him, shutting away brown eyes watery with unshed tears. Another attendant rolled back one of the sleeves of his robe.

He reached a veiny arm into the urn. The crowd grew even quieter somehow, everyone seeming to hold their breath as they watched.

After a moment, he withdrew his hand. He held a shard of bright blue pottery high in the air.

"What's it say?" a young boy blurted. Many heads swiveled to the boy, then immediately returned to the kingly figure.

The first attendant removed the blindfold. The king lowered his arm to read, then dropped the bit of pottery. It shattered against the stone dais. He staggered backward, clutching at air. The two attendants threw themselves at the old man, propping him up.

After a few seconds, the king straightened himself. He took a deep breath, then let his eyes rove the crowd again. This time, the tears flowed freely. "Princess Callista has been chosen as our next sacrifice to the beast." His voice quavered at the end, and he sagged backward, this time shoving his attendants away and leaning against a railing, staring at the ground as the crowd exploded with noise.

The tumult of the crowd spooked our horses. Tobias's mount tossed her head, and mine stepped back several feet before I got him under control.

The king stepped forward, eyes lowered as he addressed the noisy throng. They quieted as he spoke. "I would offer all the gold and treasure in my vaults, every book in my library, to anyone who could spare my daughter this fate. But I am a just king, and I put my own name and that of my daughter into the urn. I knew that at any time, it could be the royal family chosen for the sacrifice."

He turned to his daughter. "My dear, I am sick inside that I shall never see your true wedding day, never hold the hand of my grandchild."

The princess turned to the crowd. She spoke so softly I had to strain to understand. Afterward, I was never certain I'd heard her correctly. "My people, if I can spare even one of you this fate, I go gratefully. I only wish we could find a way to break the cycle of death and anguish."

"Prepare my daughter for the sacrifice." This seemed to be the end of the king's strength. He collapsed into tears and had to be helped down the dais by several servants.

Two women in white robes came to lead the daughter away. The princess met my gaze as she left, her face expressionless as she studied me with somber, stormy gray eyes.

"What is the meaning of all this?" I spoke louder than I'd meant to, turning several heads.

A man with red hair and a dusting of freckles glanced up from beneath a broad straw hat. He shook his head. "According to our laws, the princess must go be married to the dragon of the lake. And her wedding gift will be a slow, painful death."

"What?" *Why would anyone commit such a barbaric practice?* My hand itched to draw my sword. I'd cut down anyone who stood in my way. I'd—

"How did all this come to be?" Tobias asked calmly. He glared daggers at me.

I nodded. *Mustn't lose my temper.* If we got driven out of

town, I didn't want it to be my fault. Again.

"A plague dragon has set up residence in our lake. That water used to be our pride. Now our sheep are dead, our children and elderly are sick, and we're past our wits end. The dragon spares us if we sacrifice one person a month."

"Aye," a woman said. "The king's men set up a lottery. Someone's chosen at random. It's only fair. I didn't know the king put his own name in, and his beloved daughter! What a king!" She wiped a finger at her eyes.

Tobias held up both hands in a placating gesture. "Now, George—"

"I'll kill it!" I drew my sword and let it flash in the bright afternoon sunlight. "Let me slay your dragon."

"George!" Tobias called again. "Saint Jupiter, this is Pamplona all over again. You know what, one spell? Slay a *dragon* you say? We're going to die. I would have liked to see the ocean one last time…"

"He's right! You don't stand half a chance, boy!" an old man shouted.

Boy? I'm twenty-seven.

Several others voiced their agreement.

"I don't see how anybody stands a half-chance against that plague dragon," the woman said. "But I'd sure like to see you try."

"And the king would surely keep his promise. He'd make you a rich man." The redhead nodded his approval. "Worth the effort. If I had a sword like that, I'd slay the dragon and ask that princess to marry me!"

"How long have I got to prepare?" I asked.

"Dawn tomorrow," the redhead said.

"She'll be dead by breakfast time," the woman added. "And poorer the world will be for it."

൙൙൙

That night, attendants prepared Princess Callista for her deadly wedding. In the early, predawn darkness, they brought her to the lake. She wore a crown of wreathed flowers and a wedding dress adorned with crystals that glittered in the flickering light of the servants' torches.

Armed and armored, I followed, determined to save the

woman and free the village from its curse. I hid behind a tree and waited as they tied her up, gripping my spear in gauntleted hands. Amid Tobias's several protests that we should flee town, he had insisted I wake him before I left. I'd agreed, but then he'd proceeded to drink *so much ale.* I'd decided to let him sleep it off. Tobias the morning after a binge was a sight to behold, and I wasn't looking for *that* brand of help.

As I watched, the servants tied the princess to a tree near the shore and left her for dead.

The cowards!

My blood boiled with rage, but there was no time to think about that. The water shifted. I charged forward to free the woman. A noxious, purple dragon rose from the water, revealing a long, snakelike body and sinuous lizard legs. As the beast darted forward to bite me, I stepped to the side and shoved my spear into its shoulder. Awful, lavender steam puffed from the wound, smelling of rotten eggs. My eyes watered.

Curious. Some sort of dark magic at work.

The dragon let out a piercing scream. Temporarily deafened, I stumbled backward. I lost my grip on the spear, which stayed embedded in the dragon. I'd wounded the monster, but not badly enough to drive it off. It retreated a few steps into the water. Ears ringing, I raced across the gray sand to the tree.

Princess Callista watched me with worried eyes. "Behind you!" she cried a second before I reached her. Her voice sounded far-off, almost tinny.

I drew my sword and turned in one fluid motion, swinging my blade. It clanked off thick scales. Cutting wouldn't do; I needed to stab as I'd done with the spear. I lunged forward, darting under the creature's arm as it struck out with a powerful talon. I aimed my sword for the foul creature's heart, but the beast smacked down on my sword, knocking the blade from my hand. I stumbled, falling forward. The creature raked its claws across my armored back.

I rolled and kicked upward, driving my boot into the monster's chin. Struggling to my feet, I grabbed the spear and *twisted.* The dragon let out another piercing howl. I leaned on the weapon, driving it deeper. With my other hand, I pulled a dagger from my belt and sliced at the leather bonds holding

Princess Callista down.

The dragon swung its tail and swept my feet out from under me. I fell backward and smacked my helmeted head against a tree. Dazed, I watched the dragon reach its serpentine neck around and grab the spear with its mouth. It yanked the point free, releasing another gush of fetid steam.

The dragon inhaled deeply. Would it exhale poisonous steam all over us?

"Princess! Your belt!"

"My... what?"

"Your belt! Hand it over!"

"You have strange timing, sir knight. I generally prefer if men—"

"For the dragon!" There really wasn't time to discuss it.

Callista removed the belt and pressed it into my hand.

Throwing myself forward, I wrapped the leather belt around the dragon's neck and cast the only spell I knew, a Pacification charm I'd been taught during my training as a Legion-Knight. I cinched the belt tight and slid off the monster's back.

The dragon writhed backward, sending up a splash of foul water. Its head snaked through the air, then flopped to the ground. Back arched, the dragon glared at me with baleful, violet eyes.

Princess Callista stepped forward, smiling. "Why, it's tame as a kitten."

"Careful." I took a protective step forward, putting myself between her and the dragon.

But the hateful glare melted away. Eyes wide, the dragon lowered its back and settled itself at the feet of the princess.

I studied the meek dragon. "It seems fond of you."

She grinned at me through messy waves of dark hair. "Well, we *are* married, are we not?" She swept her hair out of her face and grabbed a loose bit of the belt that hung free, giving it a gentle tug. "Come along, husband."

"I'm not sure that's a good idea, milady."

"Then you'd best gather your things and walk with me, sir knight."

Knowing better than to argue with the princess, I

acquiesced. We strode back into town, perhaps the strangest trio to ever travel that road. A battered knight, a disheveled princess, and a gentle, wounded dragon.

A small parade of townspeople formed behind us as we returned to the square. Tobias watched from a balcony as we passed the inn. I caught his eye and grinned fiercely, and he responded with a rueful smile.

Someone must have run ahead to alert the king, because he waited on the dais for us. "What do you mean by bringing that beast inside our walls?" The king's voice shook as he glared at me. He studied the three of us intently. "Have you saved my daughter, or doomed us all?"

I stepped up to the purple dragon and slipped the end of the belt from the princess's fingers. Taking a deep breath, I removed the makeshift collar from around the dragon's neck. Its eyes flared, but before it could do anything, I shoved my gauntleted hand down its gullet. The dragon rocked backward in surprise, and I staggered free, hand emerging with a purple gem the size of my fist. I let it fall to the ground, where it lay smoking on the packed dirt of the town square.

"This dragon ate a cursed gemstone," I announced. "That's why it was polluting earth and air."

The dragon threw back its head, releasing an inferno toward the sky. I could feel the heat warming the metal of my armor. As the fire blazed, the beast's scales changed from purple to a beautiful sapphire blue. Afterward, it dropped at my feet, unmoving.

A cry cut the sudden silence. "Sir George has slain the beast!"

"A cheer for George the Dragon Killer!" another voice added.

The crowd roared in exultation.

"You have saved my daughter and freed my city." The king threw his arms wide. "For that, we are eternally grateful. Anything in my vault is yours."

I glanced at Callista. "I have a different treasure in mind."

The princess rolled her eyes at me, but grinned.

As the crowd dispersed, I studied the beast. Dragons are resilient. Removing the gem shouldn't have been a death sentence.

The dragon glanced up without moving its head, and its lip twitched with an almost imperceptible smile as it gave me a slow wink.

DREAMS AND NIGHTMARES
Luna R. Fuhrman

"They've tried to kill you nine times," my uncle said. He tossed the sword I'd dropped back at my feet. "If you don't focus, the tenth might be your end."

I gritted my teeth. Once again, my anger against the Voran had consumed me and I'd lost focus.

"Don't let vengeful thoughts take control," he said. "Focus. Don't fixate."

"Why do I have to learn combat?" I asked and picked up my sword. "My magic is strong enough."

Uncle sighed and shook his head.

"Your magic is dangerous, Kelsai. You should only use it when absolutely necessary. Now, try again."

With my feet slightly apart, I raised my sword. Uncle lunged forward. But this time, I evaded his attack and swiped his feet out from under him. He landed face up on the ground and laughed.

"Very good," he said, taking the hand I offered him.

After that, we took a break to get a drink of water. As I gulped mine down, I noticed a young girl working in the nearby field. Her face was hollowed out from starvation—all too common since the Voran's taxes often required families to give up half their food reserves when they didn't have enough coin. Hatred tingled in my fingertips as I thought about the council of five sorcerers that ruled over Roveles. They wielded their unrivaled magic against the people like it was their birthright. They were hungry for power and didn't care about the lives destroyed to obtain more.

"I wish our people didn't suffer," I said.

Uncle came up beside me and placed a hand on my shoulder. "Have hope. You'll fulfill the prophecy and end that suffering." His hand dropped, and he morphed into training mode. "Thirty seconds, then back to work."

My training started two years ago after my dream. The memory was still vivid in my mind. I was in the Voran's council chamber. They stood in a circle around me. And one by one they died under my gaze until the last and strongest sorcerer remained.

Lox. The vilest and most infamous of the Voran. Four years earlier, he'd killed an entire rebel group with one wave of his magic, including my parents. At the end of the dream, I stabbed him in the heart.

Apparently, Lox had experienced the same dream that night, which made it a prophecy revealed through his magic. I was *destined* to kill the Voran, so they'd sent assassins to kill me first. Unfortunately for them, I'd overcome all their attempts, thanks to my uncle. He trained me in combat and sorcery, though he didn't have magic himself. Not many people did.

We were all we had left. So we protected each other.

The memory shattered when a high-pitched whistle preceded an arrow barely missing my left shoulder. My eyes shot to a tall woman stepping from the shadows. She wore all black and had a raven tattoo next to her left eye. The symbol of assassins.

My lips formed into a grin. "I guess you're lucky number ten," I said and drew my sword.

The woman sneered and launched herself at me. I blocked and counter-attacked. We struck and countered back and forth, surprisingly even-matched.

"They were right. You *are* annoying," she said through clinched teeth.

She struck again and twisted her sword in a circle. My wrist bent at an awkward angle, and my sword flew away. Uncle stepped in to block her attack while I retrieved it.

The three of us danced around each other, metal flying and feet kicking. I thought we had her, then she threw a spin kick, hitting Uncle squarely in the chest. He flew backwards. I cried out and raced towards him, but something stopped me. Red light glowed around my core. My pulse raced like a galloping horse. The red yanked me backwards. I soared through the air and slammed into a tree. I groaned and blinked until my vision refocused.

The assassin sauntered toward me. Red light haloed her right hand. Her magic squeezed my chest and stifled my breaths.

"Sending a sorceress to kill me, the Voran must be scared."

I tried to stand, but couldn't move. Her magic covered me like a lead blanket. My sword was within reach, but my arms were pinned to my sides.

She stepped closer. Her eyes glowed red, matching her magic. She slid a dagger out and twirled it in her hand. Panic seared through me. I couldn't die. Not before I killed the Voran.

The sorceress stood over me.

A shout came from behind her. Uncle charged, sword raised. She whirled around in time to immobilize him with her magic, then she plunged the dagger into his chest.

I cried out. Uncle's eyes widened as he stumbled back and fell.

"No!" I screamed and stood, finally free of the sorceress' magic. I ran to him. "I need you. Stay with me. Please."

He laid a shaky hand over mine. "You don't need me. It's time. Fulfill your destiny."

His eyes closed. Tears poured down my face. It couldn't be time, not without him. I turned to the woman. The other assassins had died by my sword. She would die by my magic.

I stood again, took a centering breath, and released my power on her. Her screams ripped through the woods as darkness consumed her.

I looked down at my uncle's body once more. Tears clung to the corners of my eyes. The Voran did this.

Uncle was right. It was time to kill them.

ುಲುಲು

Shadows concealed me where I perched in the rafters. The Voran mingled in the center of the room as advisers and servants exited.

The council chamber I'd sneaked into perfectly displayed their greed. Gold glimmered in everything. This was the kind of extravagance that starved the people of Roveles.

I waited until only the five members of the Voran remained, then I swung down from the rafters and dropped in front of them. Slowly, I lifted my eyes. Their initial shock gave way to grim recognition. They loomed over me like mountains casting judgment on the forest below.

"Hello, Kelsai," Lox said, his voice as menacing as his blue eyes. Technically, each member of the council was equal in political power, but everyone knew *he* was the unofficial leader.

"Always a pleasure Lox," I said. "Had any good dreams lately?"

He laughed, but I saw the flash of nervousness in his eyes. "Nice of you to come to us. Now I can kill you myself."

Blue light exploded from his hands. I slid under it. A column exploded behind me. I hurled a throwing star at him, and it sank into his thigh.

"You are nothing compared to us!" Lox bellowed.

"I am your destiny!" I yelled back.

His next beam of magic licked my arm, searing across my bicep. Two other Voran joined the fight, both with telekinesis. But whatever they sent at me, I deflected with throwing stars. Streams of yellow and red mixed together as the fourth and fifth sorcerers attacked.

I imagined I was water, flowing between their bright magic — the paralysis of the yellow, the control of the red, and the destruction of the blue. Every now and then, a stray beam brushed my finger or singed my hair, but I managed to evade the brunt of their force. Hatred bubbled in me as I locked eyes with Lox. He'd murdered my parents. He'd torn our kingdom to shreds. Everything faded from my attention except that monster. I lunged for him.

"You're going to have to try harder if you want to prevent your prophecy from—"

Something barreled into my back. Yellow light engulfed me. Just before the paralysis took hold, I turned to see Sneedle and his long, pointed nose. Lox's right-hand man. He smiled, and my body fell with a loud *thunk*.

The world went into slow motion. Lox's laugh echoed through the room. The Voran circled around me, five smug faces beaming at a helpless girl.

Focus. Don't fixate. How many times had Uncle told me that? I'd been so fixated on destroying Lox that I'd lost focus of the battle. I hadn't noticed Sneedle behind me. And now his magic seeped through my limbs, like slow, paralyzing tar.

Flashbacks of watching Uncle die while I couldn't move brought new tears.

Lox knelt down over me. "It appears my prophecies aren't infallible. A mistake I can live with." A jeweled dagger appeared in his hand.

Every muscle in my body raged, but Sneedle's magic had taken control. The paralysis swallowed my scream. Tears streamed down my cheeks, and I could do nothing to stop them. I imagined hundreds of people suffering from Sneedle's magic— all forced into submission as guards stole everything they owned. I thought of them using the paralysis against rebels during torture. The agonizing pain they suffered in silence.

No. This was not how it would end.

Uncle's warning rang in my head. *Only use your magic when absolutely necessary.*

Power stirred in my chest, a slight vibration roaring to life. I'd survived every time the Voran had tried to kill me. I'd survive again.

Black lines appeared under my pale arms, and Lox's eyes widened. He clearly didn't know I had magic. The dagger trembled. He should have plunged it into me right then. Lox fell away, startled by the change. The rest of the Voran stumbled back.

A glittering black fog formed around me. Bolts of light snapped through it.

"What… is it?" one of them asked.

Another fumbled farther backward. "I've never seen…"

The fog turned into a dense cloud, pushing the men back until they hit the walls.

One by one, the sorcerers screamed. They had ruled this kingdom into ruins, and now their chorus of pleas and desperate bargains filled the chamber. Over me, terrifying images of vicious beasts, armies in red-stained armor, and burning castles floated by. The nightmares of each council member. For that was my magic. It turned worst nightmares into reality.

My fingers twitched. As if I'd been splashed with cold water, feeling rushed back into every part of me. I lifted each limb to ensure it worked. When I sat up, I saw Sneedle crouched against the wall in front of me, mouth open mid-scream. Eyes wide as silver coins. Skin pale as snow as he stared into the black cloud. It must be horrible to die of fright.

The rest of the Voran soon shared Sneedle's fate until only Lox remained.

My eyes narrowed, like a predator spotting its prey. I funneled all my magic at him, and blackness poured from me.

Blue flashed in front of the sorcerer—a wall of magic to block my own. Except the wall didn't just *block* my magic. It reflected it back at me, and I ducked too late.

The world melted into a starless night.

I reached out for something to hold onto—anything to ground me. But I found only black and ice-cold terror.

My breathing turned shallow and fast. Lox's laugh roared in my ears. I couldn't tell if it was real or the illusion. His translucent face appeared before me, and he drove the dagger into my heart.

The shadows in the black shifted. Instead of Lox's face, they revealed a family sharing a single apple for dinner. Children being dragged to war. Innocent people beaten and mocked. The scenes flashed before me. They confirmed my failure. I wasn't strong enough to kill Lox. He'd live forever and thousands would suffer because I couldn't fulfill my destiny.

It was my worst nightmare.

I clenched my eyes shut.

"Kelsai."

The voice called like a lullaby. I opened my eyes to see Uncle standing before me. Or rather, the dream version of Uncle.

"Have hope," he said.

Those two words were his most important lesson. My magic was dangerous. It brought despair. And he'd said the only way to keep it from devouring me was to have hope.

Uncle faded into new images. Young parents laughing as kids played in the garden. Neighbors greeting each other with smiles. Authority that protects instead of suppresses. A kind king who spends his days trying to ease the troubles of his people.

That was my hope.

I stood.

The dark receded from me, pooling in my fingertips. I

unleashed it—all of it—at Lox, and it shattered his blue barrier. As it faded away, the darkness swallowed his terrified scream.

"Please! You don't have to do this," he pleaded, but he wasn't looking at me. At least, not at the *real* me.

Standing before him in an eerie glow stood my nightmare image. The apparition wore an insidious smirk I'd never donned in my life. It held an eerie version of the dagger Lox had tried to kill me with.

I was *his* worst nightmare.

The color drained from his face. He crumpled to the ground. The most influential man in the kingdom, nothing more than a coward. The white illusion floated toward him as I picked up the real dagger.

I stepped behind the apparition. Lox didn't notice me.

"You destroyed this kingdom and its people," I said. The apparition's face remained frozen with that smirk. "Your greed drained the land of hope, but your reign of terror is over. We will overcome."

The nightmare washed over me as I strode through the veil, and I plunged the dagger into Lox's heart.

The black cloud around me erupted into a thunderstorm. Wind tore through me. I released the dagger and covered my face. With Lox's last breath, the hurricane abated, and I pulled all my magic back in. Lox opened his mouth to speak, but no words came out. His eyes remained open, frozen with fear.

I rose and surveyed the room. Five dead men. Part of me despised my magic and its destruction. I had no desire to crush others to feel powerful. That's where the Voran and I differed. My vision, what I hoped the world would be now, came back into my mind. I smiled as I turned and left the nightmare behind.

Hope would live again. Though, I suspected it had never really died.

HOLD
Emily Hayse

Hope is more painful than anything. More than dying, more than knowing—knowing beyond a doubt you've been beaten. It's a yearning in the stomach, or a gnawing in the heart.

Almost like happiness, only you can't bring yourself to cry.

"What're you lookin' at the scanner again for?" Gar's looking over my shoulder. I set down the scanner and shift my position to peer at him. The scruff and dirt on his face are so mingled, all that's really clear are his pale, blue eyes. Tired. Deadened.

"Just in case."

"Got advice for you, kid. Don't get your hopes up." He snaps the top off his canteen and takes a small swallow.

By the slosh, I know he's as low as I am.

"You know, we have almost a day left." I can't quite keep the reproach out of my voice.

Gar holds up a couple strong, knotty fingers. "It's ten past the day-change mark. Since it takes about ten hours to cross the gully and climb this ridge, that only leaves about four more hours for him to show up on the scanner. The odds are bad, kid."

I shift away from him, the muzzle of my rifle scraping against the hard ground. "Doesn't mean it can't happen," I mutter. But he has a point.

We were nearing the end of our extraction time a week ago when the dust-eater—our surface terrain vehicle—broke down. Within hours, the Agagians moved in across the ridge. Coincidence, perhaps, but unnerving.

In the light of the hot sun, I don't even need a scanner to observe them. I catch the flash of their equipment, their armored vehicles, their heavy airship. Word is, they're more like a gang than a research outfit.

Our guide, Damian, who went for help after we broke down, had scars from dealings with them. Some of the mercs at the barracks said he was Agagian himself—he spoke their language—but I don't believe it. We got along fine, the two of us. He was closest to me in age, and we knew this planet's territory best.

He took me aside as he prepared to leave, made me promise to hold out. "They'll tell you it's dangerous, and it's true. I get caught, I may or may not be able to worm my way out of death. I could break a leg or lose my water, and that'd be it. But don't let it make you doubt. I got you in, I'll get you out, you hear?"

I promised him. And I don't break promises.

ଓଓଓ

I watch the gully and the dry riverbed that runs down from the opposite ridge like a hawk all day, even when I'm not on duty.

We're four hours out from sunset, and there's been no sign of him. Not by sight. Not by scanner.

About then, Marcus comes up from his temporary lab looking like he's a member of the mercenary guard, not the one they're here to protect—tall, with a deep, thick accent, hair cut longish, and tattoos covering both arms. Keeps his hydroterrachrometer in his back pocket, as if it isn't a delicate and very expensive instrument.

He jerks his bandanna off his face, down around his neck. Most of us are used to eating dust and only cover our faces when there's a storm, but I think he's got a lung condition.

"He ain't coming. Not unless he's bringing the Agagians back with him." He looks pointedly at the scanner in my hand. "Do you know how much a man like me's worth?"

I bristle. "What do you have against him?"

"Got nothing against him. But let me ask you, kid. Suppose you know the people from the other planet, you know both languages. One side has a valuable scientist, knowledge worth a lot. The other, money and ambition. You're on your own. You can risk your life to get the scientist out, no extra favors for you, or you can keep your life and sell 'em out for millions. Which would you pick?"

"Cowards sell out." I spit. "Damian's not a coward."

"Smart men sell out. Especially men who can navigate both sides."

"Then why'd you let him go? Why not send Gar? Or two of

us?"

Marcus gives a laugh. Humorless. "You've got a lot to learn, don't you? Another man for what? We need 'em here, and you know it."

Gar shakes his curly head. "We were almost as good as dead when the trans broke. Damian was just a—a fool's hope. All our chances are spent. That's all there is to it."

"Time's not up yet," I remind him. I heft the gun's sling back over my shoulder where it's slipping. I got this commission—my first real commission without Dad—at barely seventeen, because I know this planet. I've been here eleven times. I'm not letting a parts failure be the end of us—it's been the end of more than one good man, true, but not on my first commission. "You'll see." I lick my parched lips, tasting dust. "Damian's coming back for us."

As I turn my back, I hear Marcus's dry laugh.

‌ಀಀಀ

There's only one other man on this mission, a mercenary named Ian. He and I sit together by the fire as the setting sun turns the horizon blood red. Oddly, Ian's the one that looks like a scientist on this team. It's crossed my mind that they might've chosen him for that very reason—as a decoy. He's got neatly brushed brown hair, cornflower eyes, and a nice ring on his finger. Even the dust gives him a kind of pathos instead of the dirty, tired look the rest of us have. But I hear he's a crack shot.

He dusts the crumbs of our pitifully meager rations off his hands and pulls something out of his breast pocket. A photograph—a beautiful blonde girl with a wry smile and the deepest brown eyes I've ever seen.

I get the feeling he wants to talk about her. "Who's that?"

"Cassandra." He says her name like it's music. "I was going to marry her."

He holds her photo in loose fingers, as if he doesn't care now if the wind carries it into the heart of the fire.

"It's not over yet."

He smiles at me sadly. He is patronizing me. "It's easier to accept it now, say goodbye while I can."

"But what if you don't need to?"

His moment of genuineness suddenly retracts. "I forget, this is your first mission. Tough." He sighs and plucks a cigarette from his breast pocket, rolling it in his fingers but not lighting it.

This is only my first mission in name. I grew up in the field, shadowing my pa during his assignments. I've been going out here more years than Ian has. But the way he says it, it's like he's brushing off my hope because I don't know a ruddy thing.

I stand up, dusting myself off. The night is bitterly cold, but I would rather face it than Ian's tragic airs. "It won't be my last." I drop these words on the ground beside him as I shove my hands in my pockets and walk off.

Out on the ridge, Gar is on watch.

The three purple moons of Paheh-Trith give everything an uneasy glow — evil, like death. I remember the first night I ever spent here. My father and I ate dry rations washed down with that warmish, orange protein drink that's standard issue for remote missions.

Somehow that sounds like a feast now. Tomorrow, we'll run out. We *might* make it another two days in this climate. *Stars, Damian. What's taking you?*

"We'll give him the night," says Gar, as if discerning my thoughts. His voice is gravelly.

"And then what?"

Gar shrugs. "Maybe charge the Agagians."

"You can't be serious. That's suicide."

"Kid, that's the point. Make the end quicker, take some of them with us. A bullet's quicker than thirst."

"Doesn't make it right, though."

"Ethics are for men who have choices. Way I see it — Marcus, too — we don't have much of a choice."

"Marcus thinks we should charge them?" I've never known such a troublesome scientist in all my life.

"Yeah." Gar gives a sniff, then turns his gaze back to the gorge and the ridge on the other side.

֎֎֎֎

I have the dawn watch. Daylight spreads its long rays across the ridges, barely edging the top of the gorge, like frosting on a cake. Dawn is my favorite time, when your cheeks are so cold you can't feel them, but you watch the world come alive and know that at least one more time, you've survived the night.

Maybe this is my last day. The thought comes to me as strong as the sun, suspended over the fading, evil-looking moons.

If it is, at least I'll be under the sun, not that deathly purple light.

I have checked the scanner at regular, ten-minute increments for the last three hours. I shade my eyes and look down at the gorge anyway. A lick of dust hangs in the air. I switch the scanner back on, and my heart sinks.

Agagian craft. Heading our way.

I wake the others. Ian wears this resigned told-you-so expression, and Gar spits contemptuously.

"That's the end." He cocks his rifle. "He's sold us."

"Why aren't they coming in the airship?"

"Same reason we can't pull out of here in one, pal." Gar gives a sharp laugh. "Can't land anything on these jumbled rocks."

"How long?" Marcus glances over at Ian.

"In that vehicle? Five hours, max."

"Time enough to charge them, ambush them halfway down." Marcus looks over to Gar.

I step forward. "What do you mean?"

"I mean," Marcus says pointedly, "that he's not getting the satisfaction of selling me out. I'd rather be dead."

"We could barricade ourselves in the bunker. We'd survive another couple days." I've heard of it done.

"And die of thirst," adds Gar.

"If this is the end, I want them to know one thing," Marcus drawls. "That I went down fighting for my life, not clawing it out in some bunker, dying of heat and dehydration."

"I can't let you." I plant my feet and cradle the rifle in my arms. "My job's to protect you. And while you're here, I'm doing just that."

"You don't want to cross me, kid." Marcus's eyes are hard.

"What will you do? Kill me?" I laugh, and it sounds terrible against the dead, dusty rocks. I may be losing it a little, but I'm angry now.

"There's worse things than dying, kid." It's not a threat, exactly. Just a callous thought.

"And giving up before our chances are spent is one of them! Any number of things could be delaying him. We have to hold out."

"Hold out? With them coming into camp? I'm all for hope, but not insanity."

He stalks away.

I can't expect help from them. So, I can quit and give in now, or I can fight them to the end.

No man's ever called me a quitter.

൦൦൦

They notice an hour later when they unpack the extra arms from the dust-eater.

I hear Gar's voice from across the camp, something about ammo, but it's Marcus who comes to me first.

"What did you do, kid?" He towers over me, and suddenly my heart's in my throat.

I muster my courage and speak straight up into his long, hard-jawed face. "I locked up the ammunition. We will not make an assault on the Agagians today."

I'm on the ground before I even realize he's punched me. I haul myself back up, my chest throbbing. The air's knocked from my lungs and I feel the impact in my teeth.

"On what grounds?" His voice echoes off the rocks.

"I am here to protect you. And I will." I eye Ian and Gar, trying to gauge whether or not they'll go for me. "I can't let you throw away your life."

"That's my choice!"

"It's your choice," I agree. Calm floods my veins as Marcus goes white with fury. "And you're going to have to go through me to do it."

I want to cry. I want *so badly* to cry, but I could never forgive myself if I broke down in front of them, so close to the end.

They mean well. Not falling into the hands of the Agagians is what we all want. And a quick death is preferable to a slow one. But they can't see. They can't see that life is still sacred, no matter what endangers it—that it's the cowards who take their own lives to spare themselves from pain, not the brave.

To have courage, to dare hope—it's worth pain, if that's how it has to be.

"Foolish boy!" He leans into my face, and his breath is hot and dry. "You talk of principle, and you know nothing about it." Disgust drips from each word.

I can see it in his eyes — he's horribly dehydrated. Probably feverish. I think we all are, now.

I reach into my belt, unhook my canteen, light as it is, and toss it in the dust at his feet. "It's yours now. And don't you ever call me foolish boy again."

He practically recoils from the canteen. "I am not taking your water."

"You're worried about dying of thirst — that'll give you another day. A day more than we'll have."

Gar and Ian stand frozen. This matter is between Marcus and me.

"I…" His words abandon him.

"I won't need it." My eyes flick to the others. "We're holing up. Move — *now*!"

I feel ten feet tall and a hundred feet distant. They obey.

॰॰॰

It's almost silent out here on the rocks. The wind plays with the dust.

The camp truly looks abandoned, as we intended.

The low hum of the vehicle climbing the gorge below us tickles my ears. I heft my gun, almost don't notice the raw sting of the places rubbed by the barrel and the stock.

I'm in position before the truck pulls up over the rim. If they try the bunker, I can take most of them out before they gun me down. Enough that Gar or Ian could take care of the rest, even from the exposed position of the bunker door.

Better if they don't have to, though.

I shift my gun and wait. We weren't meant to be killers or to die in this forsaken, rocky place.

We're about to do both.

The truck grinds to a halt, suddenly blurs before my eyes. I blink, trying to clear my vision. Now is *not* the time to lose it. *Hold it together a few more minutes. You'll only need that long.*

My vision — no, just the truck — blurs more, and I realize it's not my eyes. The vehicle is no longer an Agagian rock climber, but a scanner-cloaked dust-eater. An old trick, but a good one.

Its door swings open.

"Gar? Marcus? Prosper? Come on boys, please tell me you're still here!" I know the voice.

I shift, my gun scraping against the rock, the only real sound in the humming around my head. My throat's thick—I can't even get his name out. But I stand, and he sees me.

THE NIGHT BEASTS
Savannah Grace

Evana shivered as she watched the Night Beasts travel alongside the rising tide.

She stood beside her small, grey cabin that crouched among the heather moors on the cliffside, holding the reins of her large draft horse, Oro. The deep twilight cast everything in a dark navy—everything except the Night Beasts. They were black on black on black.

The ink-drop creatures burned their way along the edge of the beach like rogue will o' the wisps, leaving dark rents behind. Legends claimed that they were cloaked fae, gliding their way across the land of the Cliff People to reach their own kingdoms that lay far beyond. And if mortals came too near, the Night Beasts captured and stole them away.

Evana had seen them take her brother from the shore six months ago.

She clenched her horse's reins tighter until the leather bit into her palm. Twins, they'd been—he'd had her face. Diederik had been her home, her heart, her safe place, he—

Was gone.

The townsfolk said he was dead, told her to give up, told her to let his memory wash out with the waves. But she knew better. He was her twin, and he was alive. Somewhere. Somehow.

And Evana had watched the beach ever since for the return of the Night Beasts.

She pressed her lips into a white line. She had no weapon, but she had something better, and in the back of her mind, she wondered if it would kill her. Ever since that dreadful night, she'd run along the shoreline, practicing. Her muscles were of iron now, and she felt half wild.

She hoped it would be enough.

Oro shifted and snorted white breath into the cold air,

tossing his head. Evana turned, grabbed a fistful of his mane, and swung herself onto the horse's broad back.

"Don't be afraid," she whispered into the great beast's ear, more to herself than to him.

The Night Beasts shrieked, a far-off call, bearing away across the dark sand into the forest beyond it. Evana dug her heels into Oro's sides. He snorted and broke off down toward the water.

I am coming, Diederik.

Girl and horse galloped alongside the edge of the ocean, throwing sand clouds up in their wake. The rents left behind by the Night Beasts smoked, and Oro's neck arched as he avoided them. Evana's hair tangled in the wind. She let him slow when they broke from the clear shoreline into the forests that ran alongside the ocean's edge.

As they entered, the smell of rotting leaves hit her nose. Her heartbeat buzzed with the adrenaline of unknown possibility and the familiar presence in the night. *Diederik.*

He had cared for her since their parents' death six years past, when she was eleven. Their ship had cascaded down the wrong side of a wave, and the townsfolk — easily suspicious, easily warded away — had pegged the twins as cursed. Born for a life of misery.

Diederik had shouldered their hard looks and became a man too soon.

Just as Evana now shouldered the forest's hard gaze and tried not to turn and run.

Farther in, the tree trunks bore the Night Beasts' blisters and scorches. Oro snorted and shied from a blackened bush, and Evana guided him toward an untouched tree. The damage would only worsen as she followed the Beasts deeper in — the horse's survival instincts would send him back to shore. Hers would not.

Hers said to find her brother.

She slid from Oro's back and looped the reins around his neck, then reached up to put her hand on his broad muzzle. His nostrils flared pink, quivering as she nodded. "Go home."

The large animal swiveled and cantered back toward the cliffside and the cabin, his heavy hoof beats thundering into the night.

Evana kept on.

The rents grew deeper as she drove farther into the forest. Instead of smelling like oaks and rotting leaves, the cold night air reeked of charcoal. It slid thin through her chest, never allowing her to quite catch her breath as she crept toward a large tree, its trunk gnarled and burnt black. She had to be close now.

What do Night Beasts look like from ten feet away?

Evana pressed her body up against the tree's rough hide. Careful not to disturb the leaves underfoot, she shifted to see around the trunk—and her breath stuck to her spine.

Night Beasts coalesced around a fire that shimmered silver. The legends were true; the fae had shed their cloaks of will o' the wisp and now loomed like sinister shadows against the background of bent trees. Smoke wafted off of their translucent, black skin, showing bleached bones underneath. Their forms were human, but sharper, edged in glass. And their eyes were voids. Terrible.

Evana felt a shiver slid from her gut and into her ribs. Would that be what it felt like if they stabbed her through the chest?

She stepped back. *I can't do this.*

But then one of the Night Beasts turned, the fire casting a silver light across the lantern swaying in its hand. Except, it wasn't a lantern. It was a cage. It *pulsed* inside, and even from so far away, Evana could feel the presence trapped within. A *human* presence.

Diederik.

A cry like a wounded bird rose up in Evana's throat, and she caught it between her teeth before it could escape.

I... I'm coming, Diederik.

Powered by the strength of her anger and fear, Evana took a trembling step out from behind her tree, and then she promptly collapsed. Her left hand landed on a still-smoking rent, and she screamed as she jerked her seared palm away. The Night Beasts spun to face her, their skeletal forms thrown into blade-sharp relief by the silver fire behind them.

They watched her. The trees watched her. The moon watched her. An osprey—lying in its death throes in the hollow of a smoking limb—watched her.

Their eyes were terrible, but she could still feel Diederik's presence, and she would not leave him now.

Evana climbed shakily to her feet and said, in a voice low and very much not her own, "I've come for my brother."

The air in the copse sucked away. One Night Beast—the one holding her brother's lantern—came forward, its jolting steps reminding her of a vulture. "Your face," it said. "Your face. We've already captured it. How come you to wear it, too?" It drew a knife, serrated and blood red, from its sheath.

Evana fought the tears of pain in her eyes as she clenched her fists—one blistered and one whole—by her sides. "I am Diederik's twin sister," she choked out, walking until she stood not ten feet from the Beast.

What did Night Beasts look like from ten feet away?

Like death. Evana swallowed the thought. "And I am here to retrieve him."

"How do you intend—"

Evana raised one hand and drew her shivering self up straighter. What did the Night Beasts love? Crescent moons, bone marrow, the scales of golden fish.

And to run.

The legends had another common thread—the Night Beasts, though terrifying, hid their weakness in their gliding cloaks of will o' the wisp. Truly, they could run but a mile before collapsing, bones broken, and that fact embittered them.

But in a human form, they could run until their host broke apart. It had to be a willing human, though—one not captured, one offering itself up to be eaten away.

For that, they would give a king's ransom.

Evana stretched her muscled arms forward into the ten-foot void that separated them. "I offer you a run," she said.

The osprey in the tree convulsed. Its feathers threw writhing shadows on the ground.

The Night Beast's eyes flickered, hungry, wanting. "A run?"

She nodded. "You will command my limbs until you've had your fill. And in return, I get my brother back."

A run, a run, a run. She could practically feel the chant whispering from fae to fae.

"What makes you think you'll survive?" The Night Beast licked its canines then put down the lantern-cage. The osprey gave another violent shudder.

Evana shuddered, too, but did not answer.

"You know that the runner has to be willing," The Night Beast said.

Evana turned her left palm up—a beckon, a promise. "I am willing."

The Night Beast lunged forward and caught her pale hand in his. Evana gasped as its black claws dug into her wrist. *Wait, too fast, I'm not prepared —*

The Beast burst into a maelstrom of black smoke, seething of midnight and malcontent. She screamed as it whirled around her, but no sound came out of her throat. The air turned into a straightjacket. Patches of black spotted her vision. She gasped for breath but inhaled the Night Beast's smoke instead.

She felt it slither around her spine, and she scraped at her throat.

Something roared in the back of her mind.

Bang.

For a blink, Evana blacked out.

Bang.

When she snapped back, she could feel the Night Beast holding the reins to her body. Settled nicely in her skin like a second rider, buzzing with adrenaline. Burning.

Gasping for breath, Evana held out her trembling arms.

The trees loomed over her, and the osprey still lay on its branch, dead now, eyes glazed.

Evana still had control of her limbs.

No, not control. Only the *thread* of control lingering in the back of her mind. All she had to do was grab it, and the Night Beast inside of her would vanish. The run would end. And Evana would lose Diederik forever.

Would she be able to let the Fae control her without forcing it to stop?

Or without dying?

I love you, brother. I will run until my heart fails if I have to. But I will not lose you again.

Evana glanced down at her legs as the Night Beast sharing

her body moved them into a runner's position. Her hands touched the cold dirt of the forest, and her feet dug against knotted roots.

The Night Beast screamed jubilantly, savagely, and the sound ripped out from her own lungs.

The dead body of the osprey fell to the ground.

Evana sprang forward.

Her calves burned with the fierce pounding of her footsteps as the Night Beast blazed through charred wood and rotting leaves. Evana sucked in air and tried to avoid the smoldering rents, but she couldn't. Not without taking full control. The Night Beast ran insatiably onward. She could feel its hunger in her bones.

This was a mistake.

They ripped through the forest and exploded from the tree line onto the black-scorched shore, and the crescent moon trembled down upon them. Evana's boots were shredded and through the soles. Her feet throbbed.

The Night Beast's excitement burned molten in her veins, trembling in her fingertips. Her legs strained. The ocean became a tangled blur of dark, frothing waves to her left, and the moors stretched out endlessly on her right. *Too fast.* The Night Beast blazed inside of her. The frigid air seared her lungs. Her mind begged her to take control again, to end the madness before it ended her.

She shoved the thought away, dug her mangled boots into the turf, and ran.

The remains of her shoes sloughed from her feet, and bits of rock tore at her heels. She cried out in pain, but the Night Beast didn't falter, it's wild madness a grating friction against her bones as it pushed her harder, faster, until her blazing footfalls burned smoldering rents into the sand.

Tears leaked from the corners of her eyes.

How far had they gone? Ten miles? Twenty? Oro would barely keep pace with her now. Evana gasped for breath, and her legs burned beneath her. Her vision blurred. Blood surely marked her trail.

Diederik.

Her body screamed, tendons ripping apart at the seams.

Pain sliced through her mangled feet. She was going to die. Her hand reached for the thread of control again—she could still—

She couldn't stop.

I am willing.

She roared as the force of the run erupted through her, and the moon lit her desperate path alongside the sea.

She could feel her mind dissolving, spiraling deeper and away. The stars looked close enough to touch.

Diederik.

His name slipped from Evana's mind just as the Night Beast finally ripped itself away. She collapsed under the weight of her returned freedom—a rag wrung out and washed up on the shore. Her mind warped and strained. The side of her face struck the sand, blood dripping from her nose to the earth and making it harder to breath. She vomited and choked. She knew her body was a shredded thing, bruised and broken, discarded by the Night Beast, but numbness had swallowed her. She couldn't feel the pain.

She couldn't feel… anything. She… couldn't… feel anything… She…

"You ran well, human."

A hand touched her cheek.

She swam among the stars.

ঌঌঌ

"Evie? Evana. *Evie.*"

Through her slitted eyelids, a face wavered before her in the silver firelight.

"Please, Evana…"

The trees were giants. She was a flea within the forest, and someone's arms were around her. *Holding* her. Her hands were cold.

"Evana, *look at me.*"

Evana opened her eyes, and her body burst. She screamed. Her sinews had sundered apart, and the cold of the night had crept deep within her bones. She was dying. Surely she was dying.

The wavering face had eyes—familiar eyes—and she recognized them right before consciousness faded from her. She stretched out her hand toward them, but it fell back, weak.

Diederik?

⁂

She awoke in a bed, swaddled in quilts and with the light of a dying moon outside the window draped across her face. Everything hurt.

"Diederik," Evana whispered.

And there he was. Her brother knelt beside her bed and took her sore, bruised hand. She squeezed his palm despite the pain.

"I did it?" she asked. Her question tore at her raw throat, and her breaths rasped.

But she was alive.

And so was—so was—

Diederik nodded, and his eyes were beautiful. "Salt and sea, Evana." He pressed their clasped hands to his forehead. "You did so good. Thank you. Thank you—I thought—"

"Diederik," she whispered, but she couldn't say anything else.

"I'm here, Evie."

He talked more after that. She saw his mouth moving, heard the words, but her exhausted mind failed to understand them. So she simply held his hand. The slant of the window-light fell across his skin, and her tears slid down to her pillow as she watched him. She'd saved him. She'd... done it.

Evana fell asleep with the sound of her brother's voice in her ears.

Everything ached... everything except her heart.

Welcome home, Diederik. I love you.

ONE FOOT IN THE GRAVE
SCE Swayne

If it weren't for the hallucinations, I could've written it off as a bad night's sleep. But sitting in my usual corner booth, fingering the butterfly bandage at my temple and waiting for my order, something about the other patrons seemed different. Or maybe *I* was different.

This greasy truck stop was like my second home. Cop habits die hard; I couldn't resist the people watching. But today, I had the distinct feeling I was missing something. Like reality was coming through on the wrong radio station and I'd lost something important in the static.

Maybe the doctors at the hospital had been wrong when they'd said I didn't have a concussion. The hallucinations were the whole reason I'd been desperate enough to actually get checked out, and I hadn't even told the doctor about them. I was fine as long as I kept my eyes moving, but if I stopped to focus on any one person, my vision swam. Shadows rushed in from my periphery, clamoring for attention. Teeth and claws and staring eyes. Too vague to be recognized, but enough to make an impression.

And it was getting worse.

This morning I had just been fuzzy, my vision going dark at the edges. But the more I saw, the more I could see, the shadows taking on more solid form. Now, in late afternoon, I heard whispers. As if seeing things wasn't bad enough… And if it wasn't from my head injury, I must just be going nuts.

"Let me know if you need anything else, okay?"

I looked up at the pretty, young waitress as she set my burger in front of me, and I immediately regretted it. I heard more than whispers this time. I heard her last words.

"Bathroom?" I croaked.

She pointed to a dark doorway.

I bolted out of my booth, down the long hall, and into a

filthy bathroom, keeping it together just long enough to throw up in the sink. I'd seen worse during my short time on the police force, but this had been different. I'd felt it. Her fear and pain, her helplessness. Sobbing and screaming, begging for mercy as the man's knife bit into her flesh. It wasn't real. It hadn't happened yet. She'd been standing right in front of me, but I'd felt her death. Her regret, her hopes, everything she had been or might become, snuffed out. *His* relief, and quick on its heels, disappointment and anger. Her death hadn't met his expectations. To get what he needed, he would have to kill again.

I rinsed my mouth, tried to clean up my mess, and all the while fought to get a grip. The prospect of losing my mind and winding up a medicated zombie for the rest of my life didn't thrill me, but it beat the alternative. If I wasn't crazy, then this was real.

Stepping back into the hall, I almost bumped into a woman. "Pardon me."

She looked at me, her eyes dark and unreadable, and this was a different kind of wrong. My vision remained steady. I didn't see or hear anything strange, or at least no stranger than her person. She didn't belong here. An elegant East Asian of uncertain age, she wore a long, white dress with a high collar and short sleeves. Dangling earrings brushed her shoulders, pearly flowers on delicate gold chains. Lotuses, I thought. Her dark hair was swept up, away from her flawless face. Everything about her looked understated but obviously expensive.

"Can I help you, ma'am?" Something had to have brought her here, probably nothing good.

A faint smile passed over her lips. "On the contrary, Shane. I am here to help *you*."

I didn't like that. I didn't like that at all. "How do you know my name?"

Her expression turned grave. "It is very dangerous to die in your dreams, you know."

I liked that even less. I'd told the doctor the truth, that I banged my head falling out of bed that morning, even though we both knew I couldn't have landed that hard. I hadn't told anyone what had come before. That I'd been having a nightmare, and all I remembered was a man with the head of an ox looming over me, and a sudden pain like being pistol-whipped.

The woman tilted her head, looking at me appraisingly. "Maybe you don't know, but the person who hired that demon to assassinate you certainly did. Lucky for you, such creatures are stupid, and he botched the job. He should have stayed to make sure you were truly dead. All he got was a piece of your soul, when a few more minutes would have given him the whole thing. It must be frightening, being caught between life and death like this."

I knew it sounded crazy. I knew better than to believe any of it. Demon assassins, really? But I felt something click. Even if I should know better, I still believed it. After the day I'd had, the way I'd felt, the things I'd seen... Caught between life and death sounded about right.

So, okay, maybe I was nuts. Maybe this woman wasn't there at all. But if I *was* crazy and this whole thing *was* a hallucination, what did it matter if I went along with it or not? And if I wasn't crazy and this was real, what could it cost if I walked away? "You say someone hired that thing to kill me? Who? How do you know?"

"The demon was... not subtle with his newfound wealth. It was obvious to my investigators that someone in the world of the living had paid him. Unfortunately, we cannot afford to arrest him yet. He has broken the laws of the underworld and must be punished, but not until we find his mortal contact." Her lovely face turned grim. "We cannot have the living hiring demons to do their dirty work. The instigator who summoned him must be found, and quickly, before his job is finished."

"Excuse me? His *job*? As in, killing me?"

"I am afraid so. He failed in his first attempt, but the payment is already his. I have no doubt he will be back."

"Can he be stopped?"

"Not until the instigator is found. But perhaps you may help us with that."

"I'm all ears."

"Adrift as you are, you could slip from your body into others' dreams. You know more than we do about the enemies you have gathered. Clear your mind and seek them out. See whose dreams are consumed with bitterness and hatred for you."

"Ma'am, I was a cop. That's gonna be a long list."

"Then make haste. Find out who ordered your death before the demon finds you again. When you have done so, call to me, and I will hear. We will take the demon into custody, and I will personally see that you are restored fully to your mortal life."

"Call to you? I don't know your name."

She walked back down the hall, her voice echoing in her wake. "Guanyin."

ംഗംഗം

Darkness had fallen by the time I reached my apartment. *Guanyin*. Everything she'd said had been insane, but I didn't have a better explanation. I flicked on my bedroom light, and my gaze immediately dropped to the blood spot on the floor where I had fallen. Where I had died in my dreams, if she was right.

Sitting on my bed, I wondered again if she'd even been real. Could my nightmare really have been a demon sent to kill me? There were plenty of people who might want me dead, sure, but hiring a demon seemed extreme.

Clear your mind and seek them out. Yeah, right. Like it could be that easy. Just slip out of my body, simple as taking off my socks. But thinking on it, I'd been feeling that sensation all day, disconnected and off-kilter, like I wasn't quite *in* my body, just following it around.

So, okay. What could a little meditation hurt? I sat on my bed, acutely aware of my own blood on the floor, and closed my eyes. I cleared my mind as though trying to fall asleep, and let it drift.

The sounds of the city faded, leaving total silence behind. I no longer felt my bed. Instead, grassy earth crunched under my feet. I didn't recall opening my eyes, but I could dimly see shapes shifting around me. Fog. Darkness, and fog.

Well. They didn't cover *this* at the academy. But now that I was here, wherever here might be, I had been given a job to do — seek out anyone who might want me dead. Lieutenant Rogers was an obvious option. His long and storied career in the force had ended abruptly when I found him and a few other veteran cops stealing drugs from the evidence lockup. In one swoop, he'd lost his side hustle, his career, his reputation, and his freedom. If anyone had reason to want me dead, it would be him.

I called him up in my mind as clearly as I could, and I felt myself drifting again, the fog clearing. I saw him now, his dream. He stood next to a presidential podium, receiving a full pardon and returning to his former position. No murder there, just gratuitous wish fulfillment. Good luck with that. I released the mental image of him and the pressroom darkened, replaced by the fog again.

I was getting the hang of this. I thought of one of the criminals I'd arrested, a small-time thug who'd tried to make it big and failed. His dream was even more gratuitous, sitting in a strip club surrounded by cash and weapons, watching a girl who defied gravity in more ways than one. With a mind that simple, it was no wonder he'd been an easy collar.

I returned to the foggy in-between, but something felt wrong. I wasn't alone. I could hear breathing out there in the darkness, low and heavy. An ox. I moved quicker now, whipping through hardened criminals and dirty cops and family members and defense attorneys and anyone else I could think of so fast it all blurred together. And every time I returned to the in-between, I could hear it getting closer. Thudding hoofbeats on the soft ground.

I had a lot of enemies, more than I'd realized, but I was running out of options. Had I missed something? It wasn't like this particular investigation method came with an instruction manual. There had to be something, some clue, some suspect. What had I missed?

I started checking on everyone I'd ever been close to—family, friends, schoolmates. There had to be someone, some connection I'd overlooked.

Stumbling into another dream, I looked myself right in the face. I had interrupted this one near the end, just in time to see myself begging for mercy, wrists tied together and bound to a chain-link fence. My ex-girlfriend Cindy stood over me, her beautiful face twisted with disgust and rage, a leash in each hand leading to a pair of massive Rottweilers. They were dream-dogs— nightmare-dogs—too big, and with way too many teeth.

"You always were a dog, Shane," she said. I'd heard that before, after every night shift, every late call that she thought had more to do with booty than duty. But what came next was new. "And you know what they say. It's a dog-eat-dog world."

She let go of the leashes, and the dogs charged forward, snarling in stereo. There's something uniquely unsettling about watching yourself being torn into tiny bloody pieces by snarling canines, even more so when it's the greatest desire of someone who once said she loved you.

I slipped out of the dream. I had my culprit, but not one I'd hoped for. I would have understood if it was almost anyone else, but we had broken up over a year ago, and I couldn't think why she would want me dead now. Back then, sure, the breakup had been a mess, but she should have had plenty of time to recover.

I rematerialized in the fog. Hot breath dampened the back of my neck.

The ox demon.

I ducked and threw myself to the ground. As I rolled away, something heavy whipped through the air behind me. I instinctively reached for my gun. Not there. "Guanyin!" I scrambled to my feet. "I found her! It's Cindy Harper!" I turned to face the demon. He was gone.

My eyes shot open, and I gasped as absent sensory input rushed back. The clamor of the city outside. The smell of dinner cooking in the apartment across the hall. The blinding bedside lamp. But when my vision adjusted, I saw Guanyin standing at the foot of my bed.

"Well done, Shane. You adapted admirably."

"Why did she do it?" I asked. I had a million other questions, including *how* she had done it, how Guanyin had gotten into my apartment, and whether my insurance would pay for the antipsychotics I clearly needed, but this seemed the most pressing. "It was ages ago."

"It takes a long time to pull off something like this. And a certain degree of psychosis to follow through. My authorities will deal with her." She reached into a silk bag hanging at her wrist and pulled out a white lotus. "Your prize, found in the demon's possession upon his arrest."

"What is that?"

"It contains the missing piece of your soul. Returning this, as it is, to its rightful place will restore you to your mortal state. No more ghostly visions or dream wandering. Everything back to normal."

I should have wanted that. But I thought of the waitress from that truck stop, the fear I'd felt as she died. Now that I knew it was coming, I could try to stop it, but without all this insanity, I wouldn't have known until it was too late. "You said you have investigators for cases like this. Corruption and bribery between the living and the dead. Could you use another detective to help with that? A living one, someone who could help you from this side?"

Something about her smile made me think she had known before she ever spoke to me in the truck stop. "I could use exactly that. One of the living, but able to stand with a foot on each side of the stream. Maintaining the balance, settling unfinished business, investigating innocent deaths." She twirled the lotus between her fingers, and it lit from within. "Are you sure you want this job? It won't be easy. It will alter your fate in ways you cannot yet imagine."

"It needs done. I'm willing to do it."

She held the blossom out to me. "Then take back your soul, and with it my blessing. I welcome you to my service."

I needed a new job anyway. People watching doesn't pay the bills.

AFTER THE WAR
Emily Grant

"We're gonna get through this."

Keegan turned from the window of passing stars to glare at Hansen. "You just make a decision, and that's that?"

Hansen rose from the bottom bunk bed and lifted his chin, crossing his arms. "It's better than making up your mind that life stinks and nothing good is ever going to happen again just because we're at war."

Keegan shook his head but didn't reply. What was there to say? How Hansen could stay positive, Keegan didn't know, but he was not built to do the same.

"At least it's not Teller's War," Hansen said.

Keegan snorted and shook his head. "No, it's just the war that everyone's saying is going to be *worse* than Teller's."

Hansen sighed.

History told of the absolute devastation that had ensued from Teller's War a hundred years ago. Starting with the planet of Teller, the Nespotans had attacked with a vengeance, bent on conquering every planet they could get their claws on. They were eventually defeated, but not before wiping out about a third of the galaxy's population.

Now the hostile reptilian race had made a return, stronger and smarter than before.

"Our city was destroyed, Hans," Keegan said, gazing out into space as their ship cruised through the darkness. "Remember the carnage?"

Hansen stared at the floor, silent.

"Remember how your sister screamed when they carried her away with one less leg?"

Hansen's intake of breath made Keegan wish he had left that part out.

"Just like I remember watching the life go out of my mom's eyes," Keegan whispered, hanging his head. "I can't believe I'll never see her again."

"But that's why we joined the fight," Hansen said. "To stop the Nespotans from causing that pain to other people." Crossing the room, he put a hand on Keegan's shoulder. "It gets better, Keeg," he said. "I know it does. This won't last forever."

Keegan looked up at him, taking a shaky breath. "It will for me."

The following silence was interrupted by a faraway whine that grew closer with every second.

"What's that?" Hansen whispered, his eyes darting to the window.

A moment later, the sound turned into a deafening crash, and the ship rocked. Keegan fell into Hansen, and both of them tumbled across the slanting floor.

"We're under attack!" Hansen yelled, trying to scramble to his feet.

Another assault. Another chance to lose things dear to Keegan's heart.

The ship was falling fast, but to where? Keegan looked out the window and only saw stars streaking by in a blur.

"How did they find us?" Hansen yelled. "Was the cloaking shield on?"

Of course the cloaking shield was on. Captain Lyle never missed a thing. But the Nespotans were known for their elusiveness, their stealth. Their technology surpassed that of almost any other race. Invisibility shield or no, they could find anybody and attack without warning. Without reserve.

That was what had happened to Keegan's home.

And it was happening again now.

A thunderous blast sounded, and the window that Keegan had been leaning against moments before shattered as a ball of fire plumed through the opening. Debris and shrapnel blasted toward them like a missile. Keegan ducked behind the edge of the bed, against the wall, avoiding the majority of the impact.

Flames consumed the room; the sprinkler system activated. "We've got to get out of here!" Keegan yelled above the noise, coughing.

No answer.

"Hansen?" Dread gripped his stomach as he looked for his

friend through the flames. *No. I can't lose him, too.*

Hansen lay a few feet away, a wall of fire between them. But it was too late. His face was burned almost beyond recognition, and flames slithered their way across his body. Blood seeped out of his mouth, and already the life was gone from his partly-opened eyes.

"No!" Keegan rasped.

The ship was still plummeting, but the sprinkler system had put the fire out, with only a few groveling flames begging for oxygen in the corners of the room. Keegan tried to crawl over to Hansen's body, but the slick, lurching floor pulled him away.

Suddenly, the ship leveled off, jerking Keegan onto his back. He lay there for a moment, panting. Captain Lyle must have managed to activate the emergency landing system. If a planet waited beneath them, they would still hit, but their ship wouldn't be decimated.

A crackly voice sounded over the intercoms. "All survivors report to the control room immediately!" Captain Lyle. So he was still alive. But his voice held a note of panic, something that Keegan had never heard from him before. It hinted that he might not even believe there were any survivors.

What about the Nespotans? Were they still attacking? Surely they weren't defeated.

Leaving Hansen's body twisted Keegan's insides, but he followed his orders and stumbled out of the room. The hallways creaked and groaned, the weak walls ready to give way at any moment.

In the control room, a handful of Keegan's fellow soldiers gathered around a table, looking about the way he felt. Ragged. Broken. Bleeding.

Keegan stopped short and gaped at the eight men before him. "This is it?" he said. "These are all the survivors?" There had been three-dozen soldiers aboard.

Captain Lyle's glistening eyes and set jaw confirmed Keegan's fears.

"Where did the Nespotans go?" Keegan asked.

"They hit us good, and we fell hard. It's a miracle I was able to get the emergency systems up. But they're miles above us now, probably laughing because they think they've beaten us."

He clenched his fists and lifted his chin.

"They have!" Anger rose in Keegan's chest. "Hansen—"

"*We're* standing here, aren't we?" Lyle snapped. "Until all of us go down, none of us are defeated, soldier. Don't give up now."

Keegan wilted, but still a fire burned in his throat. His best friend had just died beside him. How dare Lyle disregard that?

"We're falling toward the planet Orian," Lyle said. "We'll hit hard, but we'll survive. And once we're down there, we'll bury our dead and start repairing the ship."

Bury our dead. Repair the ship.

Things had changed so fast. Already Keegan's last moments with Hansen felt like days ago.

"This battle is not over." Lyle's voice was firm and determined. Ferocity burned in his eyes as he looked hard at each of his men. "We *will* keep fighting."

It took all Keegan had not to scoff. This was *not* going to get better.

The men prepared for impact, and a few minutes later the ship made a rough, but adequate, landing.

A look out the window told Keegan that they rested on the outskirts of a big city. Sleek skyscrapers rose up nearby, small ships buzzing between them as if nothing had happened. Keegan bolted for the door of the ship as soon it lowered. He needed air. To get out of these walls and away from the destruction. From the loss.

He ran without a destination, panting, tears running down his face. He skidded to a clumsy stop when he almost stepped on a computer screen embedded in the ground. Blinking tears away, he looked out to see hundreds of other screens just like it, planted flat in the soil in long, neat rows.

A graveyard. Of course. That was *just* what he needed to see. A reminder that people die and wars are lost and things are changed that can never go back to the way they were.

Maybe this would be a good place to end the pain.

The thought surprised Keegan. It was not the first time he had considered it in the past weeks; but its return was potent, urgent. Now. Now was the time.

Keegan felt for his blaster on his belt.

His heart picking up speed, he walked through the rows of screens marking the graves. *Get far away. Don't let anyone try to stop you.*

His stomach lurched. Did he really have the nerve to do this?

You have nothing left. This is best.

He fell to his knees. Mind racing, he curled his shaking fingers around his blaster. He usually used the weapon for long-range combat. How would it work only a few inches away from its target?

At least it would make this a short process.

Lightheaded, he leaned forward, his hand pressed into the dirt beside one of the grave screens. He only needed to gather his strength so he could hold the blaster still for a clean shot.

His fingers brushed the screen beside them, lighting the monitor up and catching his attention. Two words stood out: *Teller's War.*

What about Teller's War? His stomach twisted at the sight of the name.

The memorial read:

Beloved Father, Husband, Brother, and Friend
JARRETT WADE
Soldier and Survivor of Teller's War
Spreader of Smiles, Lover of Life.

This man had survived the worst war in history.

Keegan calculated the dates of birth and death in his head. Jarrett Wade had lived to be eighty-eight years old. Certainly far past his time in the war.

How could somebody go on with life after such trauma? Keegan had heard the horror stories told by men who had fought in Teller's War. Told by mere citizens who had lived during that time. The state of his city's destruction was nothing compared to the things that they had seen. It was said that everybody lost someone.

What had Jarrett lost?

Keegan couldn't look away from the words on the screen. He felt something of a kinship with this man who rested six feet beneath him, whose experience may have been so similar to his own.

"What did you go through?" Keegan whispered. "Who did you have to say goodbye to?"

He glanced at the grave beside Jarrett's. The name was Rhetta Wade.

She'd died the same year the war had started.

Something stirred in Keegan's heart. This man, this soldier, had been through hell. He'd been scarred, his life torn apart by war.

Yet he had found happiness.

Keegan stared at the words *Lover of Life*. For fifty-some-odd years after the war's end, Jarrett was known as a spreader of smiles, a lover of life. This was how people remembered him.

A tear slipped from the corner of Keegan's eye.

He felt victory for this man. Somehow, even in the aftermath of all that he had gone through, he had found a happy ending.

The blaster grew heavy in Keegan's hand. He looked at it for a moment and swallowed hard.

His mother was gone. His home was gone. Now his best friend was gone. Things would never be the same. And who knew what else he might lose before this war was over?

Lover of Life. The words whispered in his mind. "How did you love life after all that pain?"

He sat in silence for several minutes.

Life had never promised to be perfect. He had no control over what happened to him— only how he responded to it. How he fought on and found a way to move forward.

Slowly, but not quite as shaky as before, Keegan stood. He looked down at the grave, his blaster hanging loosely between his fingers. "Okay," he whispered. "Okay."

"Hey, soldier!" Captain Lyle's faraway voice drifted to him from the crash site. "Come on, we need your help over here!"

Keegan turned and nodded. Looking at the grave one more time, he took a deep breath. "If you could keep living after Teller's War, I can keep living, too." His lip trembled, and his heart felt heavy. It was a strange sensation—as if relief carried a new weight of its own.

The ache deep within him remained. Perhaps it always would. But this moment would not last forever.

"Thank you, Jarrett," Keegan said, tears trickling down his

face as he returned his blaster to his belt. "You saved my life."

This war would end. And for as long as Keegan still breathed, that hope would keep him fighting.

STORMS OF THE HEART
Laura L. Zimmerman

Streaks of sweet tangerine melted into cerulean waves, the setting sun becoming one with the ocean. If Hazel squinted just right, the edge of the water disappeared until her body floated as if it were underwater.

She sighed, tasting the briny dew on her tongue. The ever-present splash of waves rocked the small vessel in a gentle lullaby.

Accompanying her father on his trading ship wasn't her favorite thing to do. What eighteen-year-old preferred that? She'd rather practice her embroidery skills.

At least she had a pretty view until they entered port the next morning.

"Good evening, darling daughter." Master Collins came to rest beside Hazel, one hip against the boat railing as he followed her gaze out to sea.

"Father." She smiled, taking in his salt and pepper hair, oversized nose, and small, amber eyes.

So different from her own appearance. She favored her mother—light hued locks and eyes that matched the deepest waters below.

Her father leaned closer. "Have you considered our last conversation?"

Hazel's insides turned to jellyfish. She swallowed. "I have. I've decided against accepting Master Raposa's proposal."

"Hazel." Her father stood tall, crossing his arms. "This is the third proposal you've received. You're of marrying age. It must happen eventually."

"Yes, but must it be to a man twice my age?"

"I never said he was old. You haven't even met him. We've been through this. Age doesn't matter. Neither does love. We marry for the good of the family. Making unions that will serve future generations. When will you accept this?"

Hazel's shoulders slumped. "But what if I'm different, Father? What if—"

"That's enough." Master Collins stepped back, his hands folded behind him. "I had a surprise, but you've forced me to spoil it. Master Raposa is aboard the ship. I've asked him to remain in his quarters until the morrow, when I announce your engagement prior to docking."

Hazel gasped.

"This is to be a celebration, daughter. Do not make me regret bringing you along." He raised a hand at her sputtered rebuttal. "This discussion is over. You will marry Master Raposa."

"But Father—"

He walked away.

Hazel looked back to the sea. The sun had set fully now, leaving her in the depths of darkness. The loss of all that she treasured.

Tears flowed freely. She stayed in her spot until the sky overhead was replete with clouds. The wind picked up, tossed her hair. Still she remained.

How can he do this to me? His only daughter?

An invisible knife pressed deeper within her chest as she choked on the agony that was to become her life. *Why?*

The heavenly expanse overhead flashed with fire.

Hazel startled and stepped back. Lightning at this hour didn't bode well. She turned to tell her father of the approaching danger.

Boom!

Thunder rattled the wooden beams beneath her, a sharp wave throwing the ship off balance. She lurched sideways, and her head slammed into the deck. Darkness clouded her vision.

She blinked, struggling to stand. The ship pitched wildly. A monster wave leaped aboard and drenched her head to toe. She slipped and fell again.

The sky lit brighter than daylight for another second. A crash of thunder reverberated in her chest.

"Father!" The single word disappeared in the chaos.

Bang!

Another wave caught the boat off guard. This one flipped her across the boat. Pounding, pounding. Her feet left the ground, her fingers grasping futilely for the railing.

Splash.

The raging water cocooned Hazel like a blanket.

She kicked, swiped, fought to stay above the surface. But her heavy gown yanked her beneath each unforgiving wave.

Why must a proper lady wear such nonsense?

"Fath—" She hacked against the water that invaded her body, stung her throat, and tried to drown her alive.

Arms above her head, she waved, battling to alert a crewman for help.

Gasp.

With one final breath, she plunged under.

Down.

Down.

Down.

She opened her eyes, swam toward the light. Her dress wrapped around her legs. The ocean did its best to suffocate her.

Hazel kicked. Screamed. Sucked in too much water. Her eyes rolled back in her head.

She rested. Relaxed. Sank.

This is it.

Then…

Hands, under her arms, yanking her to the surface.

She broke the top of the waves, gasping and panting. Begging the cool, fresh air to fill her, to breathe new life into her soul.

Hands pounded her back as she coughed and treaded water. She lifted her head to thank whatever crew member had saved her, but—

Her gaze connected with silver eyes. Dark curls stuck to brown skin, wrapping around strong, bare shoulders. A square jaw and a smile on a boy about her age.

"Who—" She coughed again. "Who are you?"

"I'm Ben." The tenor of his voice was tight with concern. "It looked like you needed help." His hands were still on her waist.

Her heart pounded like those ridiculous toy steam-engine trains. "Um, thank you."

She attempted to push his hands away but immediately started sinking.

"Here, let me help you." He began pulling her dress off.

"I beg your pardon!" Her voice was far too high-pitched to be lady-like, but she didn't care.

Ben stopped. "You won't make it to shore with all this fabric. You need to lose it."

"But that's not decent. How can I—"

"Would you rather be decent or alive?"

Hazel's mouth gaped like the surrounding fish. "Fine." She pushed at him again. "I'll do it."

He still had to help her so she didn't sink, but eventually she got her ankle-length dress off. All that remained were her bloomers, stockings, undershirt, and corset—far too little clothing for a proper lady. Shivers coursed through her body.

The two swam toward the shore, Ben doing most of the work. Finally, they climbed across the sand. Ben flopped onto his back, his breaths coming in large gulps. Hazel, however, lay on her side, sipping as much air into her lungs as she could. Corsets were woman-kind's bane of existence.

After her head stopped swimming, she opened her eyes and caught sight of the calm water. No sign of a boat anywhere. "Where... Where are we?"

Ben's brow scrunched together. "Haverton."

"Haverton? I've never heard of such a place." She jumped to her feet and ran to the edge of the water to get a better look at the nothing before her.

"There is no other town for hundreds of miles, miss. Where else would you be?"

"I was on my father's boat, headed back home. To Milford."

He shook his head. "Never heard of a place like that." He glanced at her clothes. "Is it a place where people dress with far too much fabric?"

Hazel crossed her arms over her belly. "I beg your pardon. I'm currently wearing far too *little* clothing, if truth be told."

Her gaze traveled down Ben. She'd caught sight of his bare chest but hadn't noticed how much of his legs also showed. In fact, he only wore a loincloth.

She averted her eyes awkwardly. "Excuse me. I didn't mean to—"

"Didn't mean to what? Look at me? How can two people

communicate if they don't look at one another?" Ben laughed, a soft rumble that melted all the tension in Hazel's muscles.

"Yes, well... I suppose I should get home now." Hazel turned to walk away.

But how, exactly?

"Which way is the road, kind sir? All I see is forest."

Ben shrugged. "I don't know what road you speak of. This is our land. Our village is just through those trees." He pointed to a group of shrubs that thinned near the back.

"What?" Hazel stomped toward the trees. "That can't be! How will I get home?"

"Well, I don't know how you even got *here*."

"Please. You don't understand. You must—"

"Benworth? Is that you?" A deep voice echoed through the trees.

Ben's eyes went wide, and he grabbed Hazel by the arm. "My father. He's chief of our village. You're not safe—"

"Benworth!" A large, burly man with a tangled beard pushed through the trees.

He was dressed the same as Ben, but with a strange, feather-filled headpiece and a staff in one hand.

His face fell, a cruel, crimson color spreading up his neck. "What's the meaning of this? Who is she?"

"Hello, Father." Ben swallowed. "We were... just coming to see you." He glanced warily at Hazel. "She was drowning, so I saved her."

"Benworth. You know better than to bring outsiders into our camp!"

"But, Father. She was going to die."

"Even so." His father scowled, walked toward them, and grabbed Hazel roughly by the arm.

She stifled a squeal, silently pleading with Ben for help.

"Father! What do you plan to do with her?" Ben ran to keep up with his father, casting Hazel a panicked gaze.

"That's for the council to decide."

Hot tears slid down Hazel's cheeks now.

Ben scratched a hand through his hair. "Let me take her, then. To the stocks. Since I'm the only one she knows."

His father grunted.

"Please, Father. She's scared."

His father stopped, shoved her toward the young man. "Fine."

Ben nodded and directed her into the village. "No worries. I'll stay with you. Promise."

"Why is he doing this? What will happen?" Hazel held her arms across her belly again, now that Ben allowed her to walk freely beside him.

He looked over his shoulder. "We've never had an outsider visit our village. Not since I've been alive."

Hazel's thoughts wandered to her own father. She broke into a new round of tears. If only they hadn't quarreled when she'd last seen him. And why had she turned down the most recent proposal? She had never even met Master Raposa. He could very well be her perfect match.

She sobbed like a child as they walked.

They arrived at the stocks minutes later. Few people wandered the village. Not many eyes to see the shame of her undress and tear-stained face. For now.

Ben placed her hands and head carefully inside the wooden platform, then closed it gently.

"I'm sorry," he whispered.

And so Hazel's time in confinement began. She reviewed her steps. How had she gotten here? Where had the storm gone? And her father's boat?

True to his word, Ben remained with her day and night. Hazel grew accustomed to their quiet talks. The way he gently fed her and kept her hydrated.

"I'll never be like my father." Ben sat on the ground, tossing rocks at his feet.

"Why not just leave?"

He shrugged. "I can't. I'm next in line to lead my people. They need a strong chief. Someone who will keep them safe. But also one who can teach them love and compassion." He skipped another rock. "My father has never had an ounce of kindness. It's my duty to change that."

Hazel sighed. "My father doesn't understand me. Refuses to listen. If he'd just give me the chance, maybe he would see that I'm my own person. I've got opinions and desires. And ideas.

Ways to change the world. For the better, like you. Not just to make money or—" She stopped. "Why do you look at me so?"

Ben smiled. "You're... different from other women. Independent. Loyal. Trustworthy." He nibbled his lip. "I... I've never met anyone like you before."

Her heart ricocheted as her gaze lingered on his dark curls. Warmth filled her belly.

She sucked in a breath. Where was this coming from?

Each time they connected, that strange feeling of sinking into the unknown pulled her deeper and deeper. But somehow, the deeper she went, the clearer she understood Ben—her truest companion. Confusion swirled inside her, doubts that she could trust a man so different from her. Yet, with this came clarity. Peace.

Ben never left her side while the village council debated her fate. He stayed with her when the villagers tossed insults. He remained faithful.

Days into her capture, Ben's father trudged toward her and yanked her from the stocks with little care. She cried out in pain as his fist wrapped in her hair.

"Father, please!" Ben fought to help her, but his father shoved him aside.

"Stand back, son. We've decided." He faced the village people. "This stranger has been found guilty of trespassing. She will face execution."

"What?" Ben leaped at his father. "No!"

Again, his father pushed him aside. "This doesn't concern you, Benworth!"

"It does!" Ben swallowed. "I love her."

His father scowled. "Spoken like a naïve child."

Hazel's heart surged to her throat.

As odd as it seemed, she loved him, too. She knew this now.

She loved his kind words, his tender heart. How he cared enough to bring her salted meat instead of the plentiful fish, because seafood made her ill. She loved how he listened to her deepest dreams. How he could finish her sentences before they even formed on her tongue.

She loved him.

How strange to develop such strong feelings in such a short

time. Yet, her heart told her this was right.

Ben locked eyes with his father. "I do. I love her. Let her go."

"I'm sorry, son. But I can't."

Ben grabbed his father's arm and struggled to free Hazel. The two of them grappled like angry bulls. After a stumble and an awkward shove, Hazel slipped free and fell to the ground, her head cracking on a sharp rock. Her world went black…

೧೯೧೯೧೯

Hazel opened her eyes, blinked.

Water pelted her face. Wind screamed wild and fierce. The sky lit overhead, and thunder rumbled all around.

She lay on the wooden deck of her father's boat. The storm raged on.

"Are you all right?"

Her gaze drifted to silver eyes. Dark curls stuck to brown skin, wrapping around strong shoulders. A square jaw and a smile that she'd seen before.

"Ben?" she barely managed to whisper.

He shook his head. "Markus. You can call me Mark." He helped her to her feet. "I saw you go in."

"You saved me?"

Mark smiled. "I suppose I did." His hands were still on her waist. Her *dressless* waist!

"Hazel. Are you all right, dear?" Her father fought to keep his jacket over his head despite the raging wind.

She nodded, her eyes never leaving Mark's.

Her father patted her shoulder. "This is Master Raposa. Your betrothed. Markus, please take her below deck so she can dress appropriately."

"Right away, sir." Mark slipped his coat over her shoulders as they shuffled toward the stairs. He tilted his head. "Have we met before?"

Hazel smiled brighter than the sun. "Perhaps… perhaps in a dream."

THE SWITCH
Rebecca Waddell

Cornstalks stretched skyward, green leaves waving in the gentle breeze. Brantley gazed at the thin clouds. The vast blue expanse called to him like a song pumping through his blood. He closed his eyes and imagined that dreamlike weightlessness of looking down on the world, not up at the sky. He savored the sensation before letting it go and returning to the crops. If Foreman Stanock caught him sky-gazing again, Father would hear about it. Then, Brantley would have more trouble than the strange longing he'd known his whole life.

With a heavy sigh, he scratched the brand on his wrist that marked him as a hybrid. Neither human nor dragon, his hybrid status was his curse and his blessing. The first from his family to show any measure of magic, it fell on Brantley to make sure the crops grew the moment he returned from school. No matter whether he'd learned how to or not. The pressure on the fifteen-year-old's shoulders weighed on him. He'd felt the sting of the switch more than once when he'd lost plants to blights.

"Get your head back on the ground, boy. I'm warning you." The gravel in Stanock's voice sent cold chills down Brantley's spine.

"Yes, sir," Brantley said, laying his hands on the drooping leaves. If rain didn't fall soon, no amount of magic would keep them from withering under the bright autumn sun. He clamped his mouth shut on the words he wanted to spit back at Stanock and let his hands warm as he connected to the plants. Eyes closed, he pictured healthy, green rows of corn like he'd practiced at school, then tensed at the whistle from the foreman's switch. Pain exploded between his shoulders.

"What do you think you're doing, boy?" Stanock demanded, his voice deathly quiet. The fetid stench of sour mead stung the teen's nose.

Eyes wide open, Brantley evaluated the brown tinged leaves

on the plant next to the one he was focused on. "They need more water."

His answer earned him a second blow. "Then you'd best go fetch it."

"I can't." Brantley winced at the tremor in his quiet words. "I don't have water magic."

"You fancy yourself above real work?" Stanock's hoarse voice didn't rise, though his arm did.

Snap.

"Think you're too good to carry buckets?"

Snap.

"I'll teach you."

Snap.

"Keep it up, boy. I'll tell your father you've done nothing." The thin switch landed with a practiced hand until blood crawled down Brantley's spine.

Before Stanock could land another lash, Brantley bolted for the bucket shed. To make any difference for the crops would take hundreds of trips, but it didn't matter. Only Mother had a chance of caring, and she was on bed rest with the latest pregnancy.

Brantley hooked four buckets to a yoke, wishing there was room for a few more. By the time he'd hiked the quarter mile down to the creek, his back had stopped bleeding. With great care not to reopen his wounds, he stripped off his tattered shirt and rinsed the blood out of it before putting it back on and filling the buckets. The cool cloth eased the raw welts that his magic would soon heal. Guilt pooled in his boots with his sweat, and he kept his eyes dutifully on the ground as he lugged water from the creek to the crops. Only after sunset did he put the buckets away and return to the sagging corn he'd worked on earlier.

Though his hybrid blood made him stronger, deep exhaustion dragged at him. Body shaking, Brantley stopped next to the rows and concentrated through his fatigue to encourage them to grow overnight. His back had fully healed by the time he finally dragged his tired body to the house to eat a cold supper and crawl into bed.

৯৯৯

For an entire week, Brantley hauled water from the creek to the crops the moment he got home from school until sunset. The entire staff did, even Stanock. His efforts kept the foreman's switch off his back, but painful welts worried Brantley less than the swiftly dropping creek levels and the ceaseless, scorching sun.

Night fell swifter each day. Only after dark did Brantley dare go to the rows of corn to encourage them to keep growing despite the weather. When he'd done all he could, he trudged home, exhausted all the way through.

"You've gotten in late every night," Jeffeth said. Older by two years, she and Brantley shared their mother's dark hair and fair complexions where the rest of their siblings took after their father's sandy hair and olive coloring.

"The crops need me." He slumped at the table and pulled his cold stew closer. Even lifting a spoon hurt.

"Yeah, but what about *you*, brother?" she asked, sitting across from him. "I saw what Stanock did last week."

A grunt was his only answer. If he didn't eat quickly, the weariness might turn his dinner into a pillow.

"He's gotten heavily into the mead," she said.

"Father?" He looked up in alarm. Father rarely drank, but his temper flared faster than lightning when he did. And it usually struck in Brantley's direction, whether he'd earned it or not.

"No. Stanock." Jeffeth crossed her arms. "You know I don't let Father drink mead when Mother isn't around to handle him. The rest of us don't heal as quick from a lashing as you."

"Not that you ever get them," he said.

Jeffeth's boot scraped on the flagstones as she kicked his shin under the table.

"Ouch." Brantley winced mostly from the surprise.

"You act like pain is only physical." Jeffeth leaned back and crossed her arms. "Tell me what's really happening with the crops. I'm the eldest."

"We need rain." He turned back to his bowl, his shin still tingling.

"Is any coming?"

Brantley shrugged. "How should I know? I can help plants

grow stronger, but I can't make water do anything. I can't make the *weather* do anything. Why doesn't anyone get that?"

"Hey, it was just a question."

"Everyone thinks I know everything about magic. They think I can do a lot of things I can't." He looked into his empty bow and muttered, "I'm not that special. I wish I wasn't different at all."

A laugh bubbled out of Jeffeth's mouth. "Oh, shut up. You whine about being special. Poor Brantley, he has magic. No one understands him. But you're right about one thing, little brother—you aren't *that* special." She took his empty bowl and pushed a full one into its place. "Eat."

He dipped his spoon into the stew without questioning her order.

"No, that's not right. Brantley, let me make one thing clear." Confidence and authority filled her command. "You *are* special. You're why the family has done as well as we have for the last couple seasons. No one ever says it, but we all know it. When you go to sleep tonight, don't forget that. When Stanock's switch finds your back again, remember that he knows you're the reason we're successful—not him, even though it is his job."

She got up from the table, swooping the second empty bowl off with her as she left the room.

ক৵ক৵

Twenty buckets scraped against mud and stones, all trying to scoop up any amount of water to carry back to the rows of corn drooping in the unseasonable heat. Brantley searched the sky and found only a few clouds scattered far away on the horizon. A telltale whistle announced that Stanock noticed where he was looking. The switch landed three times fast followed by a hollow thump that knocked the breath out of Brantley's lungs. A muddy bucket clattered to the dried-up streambed at his feet.

"Pick it up and stop shirking," the foreman growled. "If you did your job, the crops wouldn't be dying."

"I'm sorry." Brantley stooped to pick up the bucket.

Stanock kicked it upstream. "I'll make you sorry," he whispered. Mead tainted his breath, the fermented sweetness oozing from his pores. His voice rose to a bellow. "Enough of this. Take what water you've gathered to the crops. The rest is up to the boy."

Brantley used the distraction of the others moving back to the fields to get away from the drunk foreman. He chased after the kicked bucket, bending once again to retrieve it.

"You're useless." The switch landed on his back. It swung down again and again, more viciously each time. "This is all your fault."

Brantley abandoned the bucket and tried to crawl away. The foreman rained blow after cutting blow. Blood dripped where once water had pooled in the dry creek bed. Straightening to his feet, Brantley scrambled up the bank, farther into the trees. Heavy footfalls and ragged puffing chased him. His heart pounded. Branches broke. Before he could outdistance the drunk foreman, he dodged around a tree and crashed headlong into a thick nettle patch. Fetid breath and the whistle of the switch falling again and again were the last things Brantley thought he'd ever experience. His eyes locked onto the darkening blue sky. Dizziness stole over him. His vision wavered. The world shimmered and blurred.

A loud crack and a deep-throated scream filled his ears at the same time that his vision cleared. He reared up with a roar, his body no longer aching from the angry foreman's abuse. Stanock let out a bellow and fell back. Fierce joy seared through Brantley as he launched up into the sky. *Impossible*. And yet, it had happened. He'd shifted into dragon form, which no hybrid was supposed to be able to do. Each stroke of his green-scaled wings took him farther into the sky. Far below, Stanock blundered through the trees back toward the house.

Bentley didn't know if this was a dying fantasy or if he was actually flying. He didn't care. He let his wings expand with the air currents that his dragon senses could taste and smell. Instinctively, he sniffed out moisture and headed for it. The sky darkened, but his altered eyesight easily spotted a large lake. Only when he landed and felt his wings settle against his back did he realize he wasn't dreaming. He really had switched into dragon form.

"How's this possible?" he asked the still lake. Crouching at the water's edge, Brantley stared into the moonlit reflection of an emerald-scaled dragon with green eyes.

"Water... the crops," he muttered. Foreclaws shattered the reflection. Brantley stepped into the lake and filled his mouth with as much water as he could hold before launching into the sky once more. No longer disoriented with the strange sensation that had plagued him his entire life, he reveled in the feeling of the ground speeding away below him. Before long, he circled over the rows of wilted corn. He noted lights and shouting coming from the house as he landed and filled the irrigation troughs with lake water. He folded his wings against his back and stumbled forward, muscles he'd never had before aching from the flight.

His vision wavered. Footfalls and voices filled his ears, coming closer. Brantley closed his eyes, nausea tearing at his stomach. Could dragons vomit?

When his vision and body returned once again, every inch of his skin ached and stung. Stars pierced the night sky, moonlight bathing the world in silver. He swiped a human hand across his eyes and groaned as he got to his feet, which were no longer scaled.

"There he is," Jeffeth called. "Stab, help our brother back to the house. And get him some clothes."

Stab swung the cloak off his shoulders and wrapped it around a shivering Brantley. "How did you change?" he asked. "You... become a dragon."

"I flew," was all Brantley could manage.

"Stop right there," Stanock growled, slurring the words. An unstoppered jug in one hand, the foreman reached for Brantley with the other.

"Hold it." Father's baritone command boomed across the open space between them and the house. Light from the kitchen silhouetted his towering figure.

"Master Avery, the boy's failed. Crops die 'cause of him," Stanock said and drank deeply from the jug.

"What happened here?" Father asked looking from three of his children to the foreman.

"Stanock beat Brantley..." Jeffeth handed Father a broken switch.

"*Beat* him?" Father's fingers curled around the stick.

"The switch is for discipline only, Master," Stanock said. "He's insolent and lazy without proper motivation."

"*No way.*" Stab stepped forward. "I saw you break that on my brother when he turned into a dragon."

"Liar," Stanock bellowed. "Master, they lie. Hybrids can't become dragons." He laughed.

"He did so. I saw him," Stab insisted.

Father held up his hand, commanding silence. "Brantley, what happened?"

With a shuddering breath, Brantley drew himself up to his full height, still leaning heavily on his brother and sister. He lifted his head until his eyes met his father's. "I flew. I don't know how, but I did. I carried water back to fill the irrigation ditches. My magic can't do anything for the crops without water. I'm not beyond carrying it myself." His strength gave out, and he sagged against his siblings.

With a single nod in the direction of his children, Master Avery turned and crossed to Stanock. He took the jug of mead from the foreman's hand and shook it. "Empty." He cast it aside. "You're right, Stanock. The crops' fate is indeed in Brantley's hands."

The drunk foreman sneered at Brantley. "See."

Father laid a hand on Stanock's shoulder. "You misunderstand me. I hired you to oversee the management of the crops and the workers. But you left it to my fifteen-year-old son to do your job. Then you beat him for it. How dare you harm one hair on his head? You're fired and banished from my property." He punctuated the pronouncement with a right hook that broke Stanock's nose. "You better leave before my son burns you to ash where you stand."

The ex-foreman glanced at Brantley, stumbled backward, then turned and ran, shrieking as blood streamed from his nose.

Father swept Brantley up in his arms. "I'm so sorry, son. I didn't know what he was doing. You have my promise it won't happen again."

"I flew," Brantley said, his eyes drifting to the piercing stars overhead.

THE DOLL GIRL
Sarah Stasik

They put me together this time with rubber bands—the kind we scavenge from old cars and vacuum cleaners—because steel wire is on ration again. I bounce with every step as I cross the courtyard to the series of fences, but some of my parts pull farther out than others, and their recoil is never gentle.

I'll fall apart again by tonight. I'm falling apart almost daily now, and I don't know if it's me or the spare parts they cobble me together within the darkness.

I try not to complain, though. We ran so low on metal once that they used wood casing to contain Lucy's human bits. Lucy doesn't go out anymore. Probably Lucy's not anywhere anymore.

Thankfully, my human bits are still sealed tight in metal. Not all titanium or even stainless steel, and there's one ugly patch job done in copper. But none of it's wood.

Jonas is waiting for me at the fence line, and we crawl through the uplift without talking. I wait as he secures it behind us.

A gun hangs from my right shoulder, clinking occasionally against the copper peeking from under my crop top. Jonas's shirt is black with a gray raven on it. Mine's green, and you can still make out the screen print letters declaring me "nobody's princess." I almost smile at the forgotten stories they tell.

Jonas pulls his empty gathering bag and gun to his shoulders. "Ready, Princess?" he asks in his soft, gravelly voice.

Like me, he still has a human voice box. But it's been repaired more than once. He also has a sense of humor. We're still human under the metal and rubber bands. That makes us dolls, which means we still have enough heart, Jonas says, and heart is how you survive.

Heart's also how you die, I tell him, but he never answers. He just winks.

Really, Jonas is infuriating. But he still wears clothes over his metal and laughs occasionally with his broken, organic voice. That's enough for me.

We slip over the wall, and then we're on the outskirts of the city. This side of suburbia was picked clean years ago. Now, most dolls spend the day skirting the city, scavenging semi-safe neighborhoods on the other side.

Jonas and I jog, moving from bushes to buildings to ditches. We head for the city, where the bots usually gather goods.

We might still be dolls, but we know where the best stuff is.

ୡଡ଼ଡ଼ଡ଼

"Split up?" Jonas asks as we approach an industrial area. We've been travelling for hours.

I nod, and we part ways on a side street with hand signals, as if we're soldiers in one of the movies they show at night in the safety base. There's a library of films that grows every year; dolls keep finding more.

A lot of the unmarred don't like soldier movies, though. They prefer romances and comedies that have nothing to do with a battle zone. A lot of the dolls, too. I don't see why. Soldiers have been fighting and crying and putting themselves back together for centuries. It's heart. It's what makes us human.

The bots don't even watch films. Or read stories. Jonas always says that's the scariest part of existence—that you can see the end of it, and it doesn't have stories.

I agree with Jonas on most things, but not this.

Still, I can't shake the thought as I slip down an alley to the back of a building.

I climb through a busted-out window, and sharp glass scrapes in a whisper across my metal arm. I hold my shirt fabric close to protect it, though there's no real need to do so.

Dolls and unmarred think Jonas and I are brave, coming into the city. But death and danger don't scare me. And I'm not afraid that one day there won't be stories, either. I'm terrified that one day I'll decide not to care.

I move through the first room, dumping anything practical into my bag. Two boxes of paperclips, tape, a tiny first aid kit. I score a half bottle of expired aspirin before moving to the door. Aspirin and bandages don't do much for me, but dolls and bots gather for everyone, including the unmarred people back at base.

The hall outside is dark, but my left eye's no longer human, so it doesn't matter. I sweep an entire corridor of rooms—mostly workshop areas—but there's not much left here. I do find a partial spool of large-gauge steel wire under a pile of moldy cloth. It fills the rest of my bag, so I turn to head back to find Jonas. A clang from a room I've already cleared stops me.

Probably just a rat, but my heart pounds with fight or flight. You heed your heart. It's what keeps you alive.

I move cautiously into the open doorway. My left eye scans the darkness. An old office chair on wheels, an empty desk, a metal organizer. The organizer had been on the desk; now it rested on the floor. Right next to a dirty pair of small, human feet.

ളളള

I make it back to the street, helping the girl through the window after me. She has a black eye, split lip, and bruises that run up under her clothes, but she's unmarred. I expected her to run from me, but she'd stayed frozen under the desk until I pulled her forth with a story. I told her about St. George the dragon slayer, and I told her the story of Kate, a girl like her who's now made of metal and rubber bands. She'd crawled out and put her hand in mine.

I put her around twelve. About five years younger than me, but a few years older than I was when I first became a doll. Jonas meets us a couple blocks away, appearing unsurprised by my tagalong.

"That'll be the third one this month," he says, nodding toward the girl.

I shrug, and he falls into step beside us. We cast shadows as long as the buildings.

"We've been out longer than I thought," I say.

Jonas holds a water bottle out to the girl. She takes it, stopping in the street to suck it dry.

"What's her story?" Jonas asks quietly while we watch.

"She hasn't talked yet. Pretty sure someone's been beating her, if not worse."

She holds the bottle tentatively out to Jonas, and he takes it.

"Someone gonna be looking for you, kid?" he asks.

Her whispered reply is almost whisked away by wind. "Monster."

Jonas's eyes—both still human—twitch, but I put a hand on his arm. "She's not talking about us."

"The ones inside the people," the girl whispers, looking over her shoulder.

Jonas curses. "She'll have been followed."

"They're always followed," I say.

He sighs, but he won't argue. We've been bringing rescues back for three years, and he never says no. I only take the ones that want to come. My inhuman left eye reminds me daily what kind of price you pay for trying to rescue the unwilling.

We're almost clear of the city when the ground in front of us is peppered with bullets, the asphalt and dirt leaping up and pinging against my legs. I push the girl back and raise my gun. Jonas is already in position, searching for something to aim at.

"You metal freakshows think you can kidnap another of ours?" The voice comes from behind a stripped-down van, and I recognize it. So does the girl.

She whimpers behind us. "No. Please, no."

"Doesn't sound like she's keen to stay," Jonas calls.

"She don't know any better," the voice answers. "Imogen, you know what happens when you aren't protected anymore. You know what these monsters do to people. Just look at them. You want to get turned into a freak?"

Imogen rocks on her feet. Out of the corner of my eye, I see her clap hands over ears. "No, no, no," she whispers.

"I see two with guns on us, plus the guy behind the van," Jonas says quietly.

"They'll have at least two more hidden behind us," I say. "That's how Adrian operates."

He breaks from his gun sight for a quick glance in my direction. I refuse to return his gaze.

"She's coming with us, Adrian," I yell.

He pops his head around the van to get a look at me, emboldened by the knowledge that we won't shoot first with unknown guns trained on us. "Who are you?"

No chance he'll recognize even my voice. Seventeen-year-old doll soldiers sound nothing like the ten-year-old girls they once were, even if they *do* still have a voice box.

"An old… friend," I say, pulling the last word into a sneer. "One that knows you have two men closing in behind, but that's not enough to stop us without hurting the girl."

"What makes you think I care about that?"

He's half out from behind the van now. Still intimidating, but not as big as I remember in my nightmares.

"Because only you get to deal the pain," I say. He steps out further. "Because you're all flesh and bone, no metal. Even though it cost you a hand."

He's completely uncovered now, including the arm that ends in a stub before the wrist. He'd cut off the prosthetic years ago, before I stumbled as an orphan into what looked like safety in the district he'd carved out and *purified*. Before I knew what Imogen knows now — that metal doesn't make a monster.

"You *do* know me," he says.

He walks forward, and Jonas shifts in anticipation. Several warning shots rip the ground behind us. Imogen screams and stumbles; Jonas takes a hand off his gun to catch her.

"No," Adrian screams. "Idiots, not the girl!"

But it's too late. Blood is pouring from Imogen's lower leg.

"Fight or flight?" Jonas asks.

"Both," I answer. "Take her and run. I'll cover you."

"I've got better metal," he says. "You run; I'll fight."

"I'm not fast enough. I'm a patchwork of bands. It won't hold carrying the extra weight and running."

Adrian is halfway to us, and there's no time to argue. Imogen's eyes are glazed and starting to close.

"Now, Jonas." I fire my gun at Adrian's feet. "I'll shoot him to pieces before any of you figure out a kill shot on me," I scream.

Adrian stops moving. Jonas shoulders his gun and scoops up Imogen. He's yards away before I realize he's even started, and bullets fly while Adrian screams at his men not to hit the girl.

I fire any direction that bullets come from while running for the cover of what used to be a restaurant.

I'm through the glass of the window and over a booth in one

leap, but my foot catches on something. My body lurches forward and snaps back, the band in my knee bringing me together with a grinding force that rattles everything in my right side. It also locks the limb in place from knee to ankle.

The shooting's stopped, and Adrian and his men are yelling across and down the street at each other. Jonas must have got away, because the voices are all headed in my direction. I roll into a sitting position and reload.

"Whoever you are, you used to be one of mine." Adrian's voice is right outside the window. "That means you know you're a sell-out. A freak. You're letting them make you one of them."

I roll over, pulling myself up on the knee that will bend. The other leg juts out behind me in an awkward lunge. At least rubber bands make me flexible.

I prop my gun on a rotting booth and meet Adrian's eyes over it. "Metal pieces don't make you a monster."

"Eventually there won't be anything left but a bot," he says.

"You get a choice."

"You'll choose life, even if it isn't one."

I don't give an answer because I don't have one. Instead, I pull the trigger. The bullet hits a pole holding up the rusted metal of an old awning, and the structure collapses and pushes him to the ground. My barrel waivers. I want to pull the trigger and end him, but if I start shooting, I'll have to kill them all. I'll have to become the monster, and I'm not ready to make that choice yet.

I pull up on the booth and scan the back of the restaurant for an exit. Adrian's men are working the awning off him as I slip out. They don't pursue me. Adrian's not stupid—he'd waste too many taking me down, even if I *am* made of rubber bands.

Plus, I'm different enough that I know it scares him. Not the metal, but the inside.

ৡৡৡ

I'm halfway through the suburbs when I catch up to Jonas. He's sitting against a wall with Imogen collapsed on his lap.

"About time," he croaks. "We're both hit."

There's blood on his raven shirt. I bend down and push the fabric up, cursing. A lucky bullet found a weak weld.

"Don't let them replace my heart," he says.

"Never. Heart's how you survive."

"Also how you die."

"Yeah, but not today."

I dump the contents of my bag and grab the wire. I hoist Imogen on my back, and Jonas helps me wrap the wire round and round, securing her to me. Making her a temporary part of me.

I pull the emergency tool kit from my pocket and slice through the denim fabric on my right leg, removing it before going to work on myself, pulling everything from the knee down off. I help Jonas stand and butt my hip against his. We secure what's left of my leg to his with wire and the thick rubber bands from my lower leg.

Jonas leans on me. My joints squeal when we move, but move we manage—on three legs.

Half a mile later, I know we won't make it. Jonas knows, too. But we keep pushing.

Imogen wakes slightly, moaning and asking, "Am I dying?" We don't answer. She passes back out before Jonas stumbles and drags us to the ground.

We're pressed together in the grass. "Did you kill Adrian?"

"No."

"Good," he says. "You're no kind of monster."

The sun has fallen, and stars twinkle overhead.

"They're pretty, huh?" Jonas pushes the words between his lips.

I nod, letting my eyelids close before opening them again with a gasp. "Yes! Stars *are* pretty."

I reach into Jonas's pocket and pull out the night flare; they're watched for when dolls don't make it home by sundown. The white-blue flame is a shooting star across the sky.

The bots find us in minutes. One thing you can rely on— things that gave all their pieces serving others keep doing the same.

They aren't monsters. They gave up that choice with the last of their humanity.

It's something I'm not ready to let go of yet.

A PLACE AMONG THE STARS
Cassia Schaar

Earth is the most beautiful thing I've ever seen from a distance. Other planets and their moons have nothing on those shifting skies, vast deserts, and polar caps. Growing up on Dysnomia, one of the Human Survival Project's thirteen space stations, I never tired of the view.

"You gonna miss it?" Oliver, my lab partner, shrugged off his white coat and held out a hand for mine.

I glanced back at the port-style window before giving him my lab coat. "I just want to touch the soil we're studying for once."

"You touch it every day."

"With gloves and a petri dish. I want to feel it when it's still a *part* of Earth. Like the sand from the deserts? We know it has to be hot when the drones collect it, but by the time it gets to us, it's cold."

"Deserts can be cold, Miranda."

I groaned. "You know what I mean."

Oliver chuckled. "I do. I want to see it, too." He tossed me my lanyard. "Did you get your medical clearance?"

"Not yet." I tightened my pony-tail and walked out with him, swiping my badge over a sensor on my way out. The lock beeped behind us.

"Do you think your sister will?" His boots echoed against aluminum floors.

"I hope so. I want to show her some of the things we've been studying. She'd love South America. The Terra Preta is phenomenal."

"I think she'd probably like South America for more than just dirt. From what you've told me, she seems more like a sunsets and beaches kind of girl." He waved a hand. "All that poetic stuff."

I nodded. We both loved our ancestors' planet, but for different reasons. I searched for the history written across the land's surface, but Halley preferred to squint a little and imagine faces in the lines of rivers and deltas.

"Speaking of," I slowed my pace as we reach another hallway, "I need to pop in and make sure she got the medicine she needed today."

Waving a goodbye to Oliver, I broke off toward Halley's unit. Her salary for teaching the kids at the station didn't cover her lifesaving pharmaceuticals, but my earnings made up the difference.

The door beeped as I swiped my card to enter. We didn't have many decorative items on the station, but Halley had covered her walls with her own digital art inspired by old National Geographic magazines and photos scientists had taken from the telescopic camera.

Across her tiny room, she laid sprawled on her bed, holding a tablet over her face. She lowered it as I entered. "Hey. How was work?"

I dropped onto the firm mattress and leaned against a tapestry of repurposed clothing hanging from the metal wall behind me. Its knots dug into my spine. "Fine. It's getting boring, though. Do you have enough meds?"

"Yeah, for the weekend. I'll need more on Monday." Halley sat up. "Why's it boring?"

"Because we're *so* close to going there for real. I'm sick of labs. We have all the clearance except medical. Pretty soon, I can study everything in person." I inhaled the stale station air. "Do you think oxygen smells different down there?"

She flicked a finger over her tablet, and it faded to black. A smirk lingered on her lips as she stood and crossed her room to the cabinets concealing a kitchenette. "Maybe if you read something other than scientific reports, you'd know that it does. Tea?"

"No, thanks. I can't wait for you to see some of the things I've worked with in the lab."

"I *do* see them." She tapped her forehead with a teaspoon. "In my imagination."

"Some of the rocks we bring up have gemstones inside. When we go down there, you and I have to find some." Halley frowned as I kept talking. "Also, sand dunes. Wouldn't it be incredible to climb a whole mountain of it? We should —"

"Miranda. It's not we." She dumped powder into a tin mug and filled it with warm water from a thermos. "It's just you."

My mouth dried. "What?"

The spoon clanked against the inside of the mug as she stirred.

"Hales, what do you mean, *just me?*"

She ran a hand over the red bandana pulling back her dark hair. "There's no way my doctor will approve a trip through the atmosphere. You know that, right?"

I tried to swallow, but it felt like swallowing sand. "You got your medical exam results?"

"Not exactly."

"Well then, you still might get approved."

She wet her lips but didn't meet my gaze. "Miranda."

"What? Why *wouldn't* you be? You're smart, you contribute to the station, you—"

Halley slammed her mug down, sloshing tea onto the counter. "I can't breathe!"

I flinched.

"Okay?" She spread out her arms. "Just two minutes ago you were asking me about my medication. Have you forgotten already? I'm not going." A cough erupted from her lungs, and she braced herself against the table to her right.

"Hales?" I stood, heart racing. I knew I hadn't triggered her condition, but I couldn't prevent the guilt gnawing at my insides.

She held up her hand as she lowered herself into a chair. "I'm… okay."

I took her place at the counter and riffled through cluttered cabinetry for her inhaler. Why couldn't she just keep things organized? Didn't she know how hard it was for anyone to help her when—

My hand closed around the smooth plastic, and I yanked it out of a box, taking paintbrushes, pens, and pill bottles with it, scattering them across the floor. Her hand was open for the medication as I passed it to her. Two puffs and her coughing fit slowed, and then it finally stopped.

"Are you okay?" I wiped down the wet mug and placed her tea in front of her.

When Halley nodded and took a sip of the watery-green liquid, I turned back to the counter to clean the spill with a crocheted rag. It smelled earthy and bitter.

I couldn't take the silence. "What are you going to do then? Stay here for the rest of your life?"

She frowned over the lip of the mug. "You say that like it's a bad thing."

"It's just... You'll be by yourself. The kids you teach will be going, your coworkers will be going, I'll be going..." Tears burned at the corners of my eyes.

"I'm not the only one who can't go. Danica has high blood pressure; Luke has that heart condition—there's more than just me."

I stared, taking in her brown eyes and the tiny freckles that dotted her nose. How much longer did I have with my little sister? The need to memorize everything about her suffocated me. "You can't stay, though. That's just... It's horrible. It's cruel!"

"*Why?*"

"Because this isn't a *life*! Aren't you going to miss the things we'll do down there?" As kids, we pretended to be the first colony resettling on Earth, discovering things our ancestors left buried in the dunes of new deserts. We imagined climbing mountains and looking up at the stars from below. "We had so many plans."

She shook her head. "Those were *your* plans." She offered a small smile, as if she could see the memories reflected in my eyes. "You made those games up. I just followed your lead."

My tears started falling. She was right. She had followed me everywhere. I assumed she'd be following me to Earth, too. Somewhere deep down, I figured she'd be miraculously approved for a lung transplant before everyone boarded the shuttle. Even now, something inside me refused to accept reality. It felt like giving up.

"Then why do you paint all those scenes?" I gestured to the curled paper on her walls.

"Because they're beautiful." She looked at one she'd crafted recently—clouds over the ocean, peaks of white gathered in strips like mountain ranges. "Isn't that enough? Maybe some people just aren't meant to live on the ground. Is that really so awful?"

"So you'll be fine here, then?" I snapped. "You'll be fine just sitting in this cell of a room, painting things you'll never actually see?"

Halley pursed her lips and gripped her mug with white knuckles. "As long as I'm breathing up here, I'll be fine."

"Life is about more than just being *fine!*" Metal shrieked as I pushed back from the table and rushed from the room, my sister calling after me. I stormed down the hall to the closest window overlooking Earth.

How could she be okay with staying here? I was so sick of metal and chemicals and filtered air. Sick of extrapolating what Earth would be like if we returned — *when* we returned. *We*. Until now, it was always *we*.

I leaned against the porthole and watched the red-orange desert sands pass by. My eyes found the Eye of the Sahara instantly — an eroded ring of rock and sand, a bullseye orienting my relation to the planet and my goal. Was there nothing at all Halley wanted to experience on Earth? Why didn't she crave it like I did?

My fingernails dug into my palms. I'd hoped for so long to move onto something better than life in a tin can. But even on Earth, life without Halley couldn't be better than this. She helped me see the universe differently — constellations instead of lines and equations, artwork carved by glaciers instead of the claw marks of time. Without her by my side, Earth would forever be a science experiment when I hoped it would be more. I hoped to be a *part* of it — that *we* would be a part of it. But without her, I wouldn't be looking at Earth. I'd be looking up, past the curtain of blue sky to where my little sister lived. At night, I'd wonder which satellite among the stars was hers. I'd rarely be right, spotting her by sheer luck just like witnessing the comet she was named after. If I waved, she wouldn't wave back. Dysnomia orbited Earth too fast to see a single person. And until we set up ground communications, we'd never even talk.

Nauseating realization tore through my gut.

She could never join me. Not without a transplant that would never happen. Give up Earth, or give up Halley? I would lose either way. How could I choose one home over the other?

Home. I blinked and looked away from the window. *Maybe some people just aren't meant to live on the ground.* When did I start seeing Dysnomia as home?

Footsteps approached and stopped just behind me. I didn't need to look to know it was Halley.

"I've always thought wind was the greatest artist," she said.

I couldn't stop the smile creeping its way across my face as I tried to see the desert through her eyes — sand swept in swirls and ripples around dark, jagged rocks. "Is that your muse? The wind?"

"One of them." Halley stepped up next to me. "You know, you can still go."

I turned to look at her, supressing cries of both joy and protest.

"I've been thinking about it a lot, for years maybe, and I don't want to hold you back," she wrapped her arms around herself. "Part of me always knew I wouldn't be able to go, and somewhere in there, I think I realized I didn't *want* to go, either."

My voice came out softer than intended. "You don't?"

She shook her head. "But I see the way you look at Earth." A smirk crept into her voice. "Like a lover."

I straightened. "I do *not*."

Halley laughed. "You know it's not gonna look like this when you get close up. The Eye of the Sahara?" She nodded toward the window. "It's a bunch of cliffs, right?"

I could picture the rocky scene captured from the drone's camera. Nothing like the view from outer space. At the same time, the marvel of the Rocky Mountains from the surface far surpassed what texture we could see through clouds. "Some things are better up close."

"Sure. But others will never be the same."

Silence stretched between us.

"I know you wouldn't be keeping me here if I stayed," I said, still staring out the window, "but I would be leaving *you* if I left."

"That's not true. You'd be returning to Earth just like our ancestors dreamed we would."

"We were born here. It can't be returning."

"I meant metaphorically."

I huffed. "I hate metaphors." Why was she pushing back now?

"If you want to go—"

"I want to go with *you*!" I spun to face her and gripped her shoulders. "Don't you see that?"

"Miranda... you know—"

"I *do* know. Which is why I'm not going, either." The weight that lifted from my shoulders was so large, I wondered if gravity on the station had malfunctioned.

Halley's eyes widened and her lips parted. "You can't be serious."

I let her go. "I'm completely serious."

She sighed. "All I want is for you to be happy, and you can't be happy here. All you've ever talked about is leaving."

"Somehow you've managed it, right? Teach me how."

"This... is what you want?"

"Of course."

Halley wrapped me in her arms. "If you change your mind, I'll understand."

I hugged her back. "Not gonna happen."

After Halley returned to her room, I stayed to watch more of the planet's revolution. I traced the rivers with my finger against the window and counted strobe-like flashes of lightning over the Pacific Ocean. Without humans, it was easy to pretend the planet was composed entirely of science. But Halley saw it as a living, breathing planet. And maybe as humanity settled back into their old cities and towns, I'd see it that way too. And when the lights begin to flicker on down below, I'll turn off the ones up here and imagine the settlements as burning embers among the coals of night.

About the Editor

Andrew Winch is the editor-in-chief of *Havok*, an online and anthology publication that provides free daily flash fiction across a variety of genres. And as a freelance editor of short and novel-length fiction, he's worked with multiple best-selling and award-winning authors as well as beginners who wouldn't know their story arc from a plot hole in the ground. All told, he's professionally wrangled nearly two million wascally words, and he's just getting started.

But when Andrew's not helping others polish *their* writing, he's creating worlds, weaving plots, and solving mysteries of his own. Amongst other things, he's also a practicing physical therapist, a father to two Tasmanian angels, a husband to a health and fitness nut, a travelling man, a fresh water aquarist, and a novice sushi chef (those last two things are mutually exclusive). You can check out his editing services, submit your own stories, or just join the party at *GoHavok.com*.

CPSIA information can be obtained
at www.ICGtesting.com
Printed in the USA
LVHW080930291020
670075LV00031B/1360

9 781949 564877